THE ANGEL
OF FIRE

THE ANGEL OF FIRE

Lena Wood

✳✳✳✳✳✳✳✳✳✳✳

Standard
PUBLISHING
Bringing The Word to Life
Cincinnati, Ohio

Project editor: Lindsay Black
Content editor: Amy Beveridge
Copy editor: Lynn Lusby Pratt
Cover and interior design: Robert Glover
Cover oil paintings: Lena Wood
Map illustration: Daniel Armstrong

Library of Congress Cataloging-in-Publication Data

Wood, Lena, 1950-
    The angel of fire / Lena Wood.
        p. cm. — (Elijah Creek & the armor of God ; bk. 6)
    Summary: Discouraged and wondering if he can ever succeed in his quest
for the armor of God, Elijah goes hiking alone and soon finds himself in a
desperate situation, in physical danger and tempted by a demon to question
God's plan.
    ISBN 0-7847-1530-0 (soft cover)
    [1. Faith—Fiction. 2. Survival—Fiction. 3. Christian life—Fiction. 4.
Friendship—Fiction.] I. Title.
    PZ7.W84973Ang 2006
    [Fic]—dc2

                                                                            2005029651

                            ISBN 0-7847-1530-0

    02 01 00 09 08 07 06   9 8 7 6 5 4 3 2 1

The god who answers by fire—he is God.

—1 Kings 18:24

Chapter 1

YOU'LL never find it. Never . . .

"SHUT! UP!" Tending my fire in Gilead on a dry, biting day in early December, I pushed the demon's words from my mind and scratched out a map in the dirt.

Over Halloween, my clan had spent a week with the Stallards on a thousand-mile search around Ireland for the sword of the Lord, only to come up empty-handed. Those raspy words from the mouth of a polite-looking book clerk named Liam still haunted me: *You'll never find it.*

The quest was once again at a dead stop. My clan had settled back into school with a kind of quiet resignation. No one accused me of leading us on a wild-goose chase across the Atlantic. No one even seemed all that upset. They just said to wait and see.

We'd exhausted Dowland's journals, swept his house, and scoured Ireland. But the rest of the clan didn't know about the voice, and I couldn't say anything about it. They'd only make matters worse: Rob would dive into research on demonology, Reece would start a round-the-clock prayer marathon, and Marcus would preach at me about the evils of voodoo. I was leader of the clan; the next move was my call. I wanted to downplay the voice in my mind. I just wanted it to go away.

The clan didn't understand that beings from the spirit world were watching my every move—watching all of us. I'd told only Dom Skidmore and Dr. Dale about what happened because I had to talk to someone or freak out. Neither of them had acted surprised, but I was still reeling. This spiritual warfare stuff was new to me. And with Mom being depressed and steering me away from the armor quest and anything related to church, I couldn't see putting another problem out on the table. Better to deal with it myself on my own terms.

So to my surprise, here I was back in Telanoo—a place I'd once dreaded but been drawn to again and again. Not that I counted on finding anything here; there was just no place left to go. God had spoken to me several times out here—the last time saying he'd give me some treasure hidden in a secret place. But so far nothing had turned up. I sure could use a word now, and I'm not afraid to say that waiting on God was beginning to wear mighty thin.

Stirring the coals with a stick, smelling my fire going cold, I planned out my final systematic sweep of Telanoo for the helmet, sword, and arm piece. I'd give special attention to the Unexplored this time, the section lying west of Devil's Cranium between Old Pilgrim's cemetery and the place where Dowland once stalked me all night hoping to steal back the helmet of salvation. My headquarters would be here in Gilead, the hidden gorge in Telanoo where I'd found carved in stone a mysterious Celtic inscription, more than a thousand years old and thirty-five hundred miles out of place.

The Stallards had suggested that this discovery would make headlines in the archaeological world and had stepped up warnings to me about antiquities hounds and other interested parties. So fame would have to wait. I didn't want hounds sniffing around Telanoo before I found the last of my armor.

In the dirt I mapped out a rough idea of the Unexplored. *Think like Dowland,* I told myself. *Where would he hide the helmet of salvation?* Marcus and I had figured out months ago that Dowland buried pieces in their opposite environments. The opposite of saved is lost, so where was lost to Dowland?

Right here, I answered my own question. *A wanderer could get lost in Telanoo easily. I have—a couple of times—and I'm a good tracker.* I studied my sketch in the dirt. *These hills don't follow a natural flow; ridges don't run parallel. The landscape doesn't make geographical sense to me.* But Stan Dowland—who didn't make much sense to me either—had been right at home here, trekking across this wasteland many a time, away from the church he'd lost, on his way to visit the daughter and grandson he also lost.

Lost. The more I pondered it, the more I realized that the helmet of salvation could very well be in Telanoo. I looked around with a satisfied nod. I'd search for it back here on my own and maintain my running regimen to keep Mom happy. Good plan. The key to finding it: think like Dowland.

I had no idea what would happen when the armor of God all came together. To be honest, I wasn't real anxious to find out. I'd seen enough old adventure and horror movies to know that when pieces to an ancient puzzle are found and fitted into place, either the sacred underground temple collapses in a heap of rubble, or creepy dead people come back to life and wreak havoc, or the volcano god gets ticked off and a whole island sinks into the sea. In space movies, the planet explodes as the last ship of ragtag rebels zooms off, inches ahead of the cloud of destruction. The result is always complete devastation with the hero escaping by the skin of his teeth—if he's lucky.

But this was real life.

Still, I pondered, *if I'm to believe the Bible, the whole planet does go up in a fireball. No survivors. Sometime before all that happens, the love in the world grows cold, and faith in God drops to an all-time low.* I looked up into the evening sky. *El-Telan-Yah? When the armor of God comes together—when I have the sword in my hand—are we talking global annihilation? Is that your plan? Because if it is, I have some things I want to do first. You've given me a taste of the world, and I sort of wanted to see more. And there's Reece . . .*

Staring down the quiet gorge—my fire the only sign of life, every rock lying pretty much the way it had for eons, every tree frozen stiff from trunk to tip—I had a hard time believing an apocalypse was imminent. My mind was quiet. I'd thought my way out of the dumps, and the demon voice had gone. I was in Gilead, far from the world's problems and close to El-Telan-Yah. The sun had sunk below the gorge's rim an hour ago. My fire sputtered. *Better not worry Mom,* I thought tiredly. I scattered the ashes and took off through the Unexplored, making sure I'd be home before darkness fell, reminding myself as I surveyed Telanoo to think like Dowland.

Chapter 2

AS long as I could remember, Mom had organized the school's Christmas Village, but this year she stepped down and was spending a lot of time ironing and watching TV. The twins knew something was wrong and got more clingy and wild by the day. Since I'd been used to taking over at Christmas, I rustled up some hot dogs and beans for them before retreating to my room. Using my secondhand Quella—compliments of Dom Skidmore—I looked up *sword* and was surprised to find it's in the Bible four hundred times. I didn't know the Bible was such a violent book. Then I recalled that a copy of the Psalms had been named *Cathach,* which means "warrior." Dr. Dale had used it on the Hill of Slane to pray against the pagans who were letting evil spirits through the veil to this world. I had a lot to learn about the Word of God.

The clues have to be in the Quella, I thought. *Stan was a preacher; he'd have checked the Bible first, wouldn't he?* I looked up *lost sword* and found zip.

The very first appearance of a sword was on the east side of Eden. It was a glittering, slashing weapon used by the cherubim to keep Adam and Eve out of the garden after the serpent talked them into sinning. Reece had told me that no one knew where the Garden of Eden was anymore, so that was no help. And even though I was a Christian, an actual sword of fire and a talking snake seemed pretty far-fetched to me. I searched some more.

In the book of Judges, I found a story about Gideon, a mighty warrior who staged a sneak attack against the Midianites, hollering, "A sword for the LORD and for Gideon!" as a battle cry. Armed only with trumpets, empty jars, and torches, Gideon and his measly three-hundred-man army surrounded the camp and threw the Midianites into such confusion that they turned swords on each other and ran in panic. Gideon didn't use an actual sword in the battle—neither did God—but they won anyway.

It grated on my nerves big time that I couldn't pick up any direction from the Quella. I'd sat there on my bed scowling to myself, *Maybe the armor pieces are east of Dowland's garden,* but then I remembered that according to his ex-wife Francine, he never had the sword. Maybe that was true. I kept having a nagging feeling that it might be buried in the dungeons under Leap Castle, hidden away by the bloody MacMerrits who'd dabbled in the dark arts and may have wanted all good magic to be stashed away from the Christians. People like that would want to hide the sword of the Lord.

Furious, I slammed my fist on the bed. Why hadn't I insisted that the Stallards let me look for the entrance to the dungeons at Leap?! It might have been there under our very noses, and we walked right over it! I sank down in a kind of

despair. It could be anywhere in the world! Or nowhere.
I wondered if not finding the sword had driven Dowland
nuts, which worried me. Because I wanted it more every
day. I couldn't get my mind off it.

When the Quella went dry for me, I took off for town in
a foul mood, roaming down Main Street crazily looking for
a clue. What greeted me was a second-rate town decking
itself out with a ton of gaudy Christmas decorations: tacky
tinsel snowflakes swinging from street lamps and colored
bulbs slung around store windows and bare trees. Cheap
plastic reindeer with lightbulb noses teetered on people's
roofs. I'd just left home where the usual carnivorous bears
and angel dolls had been dug out and set around all over the
place in pairs—like dating couples. Silly. I was never crazy
about the whole showy mess in the first place. But now that
I understood Christmas was about God in a manger in the
Middle East two thousand years ago, the holiday fluff grated
on me even more. What was wrong with people anyway?

Then I turned the corner and was thrown back by the
tackiest decoration I'd ever seen: a gigantic inflatable Santa
Claus, almost twenty feet high, tethered by boat rope and
steel stakes to the courtyard in front of the town library.
That red and white eyesore—wide-eyed and reeling and
grinning like an idiot—hogged the whole downtown.

I huffed and walked on past the Blessed Assembly of the
Full Gospel of the Holy Ghost, Magdeline's only surviving
church. Its dusty, unlit storefront window had a plain

wooden nativity set and a scroll across the top that said "PEACE." I stood in front of the dim window and wondered if any of these members had gone to Old Pilgrim Church or had seen the armor of God.

Winding back toward home, I took the side street past The Crystal See, a seedy-looking cottage with dark windows and hardly any decorations except for two faded plastic angels—each holding swords—on either side of the door.

The next morning I left early and slipped into Florence's Greasy Cup, knowing I'd show up at school later smelling like bacon and rotgut coffee—hazards of the job. It didn't matter. I'd forgotten to shower anyway.

There were the Romeos—Walter, Obie, and Charlie—in the same booth as always. I sat in the booth behind them and ordered bacon, grits, and coffee. Nodding hello, I asked how things were going. We exchanged a few lines about the Kate Dowland case again. They knew that Francine had materialized from the dead after decades but were foggy on exactly why, which suited me. I didn't want people talking about anything related to my quest. Whether townspeople thought we were a bunch of silly kids on a treasure hunt or whether God had drawn some veil over their minds, I didn't know and didn't care.

"Guess you know Old Pilgrim Church is history," I said, stirring a bunch of sugar into my coffee. "By next summer it will be a sand volleyball court."

They went off on a tangent about how reclaiming old real estate can rejuvenate the economy.

I asked who started the church, who named it Old Pilgrim, and why, hoping to steer the conversation to a certain relic that once stood inside. Charlie gave me the rundown: "Psh!" he flapped his hand at me. "Some Indian legend about teachers who came from the four directions with great lessons, calling themselves pilgrims."

My heart took a leap, but I stayed cool and just nodded. "Pilgrims, huh?" I knew the legend of the Four Teachers, the People of the Light teaching their medicine ways. Add that to my secret discovery of the Celtic inscription in Gilead, and I deduced that the teacher from the East might well have been Brendan the Navigator or one of the other *peregrini.* History was coming together right under my nose.

Charlie said, "The same man who helped start the church and named it Old Pilgrim after the legends also built The Castle. A world-traveling politician."

The Romeos debated the age of the church—a hundred, a hundred and fifty years before its doors closed forever— then took off on how The Castle was the last of the original houses in Magdeline, how that was a crying shame. They went on reminiscing about bygone buildings and the loss of The Roanoke and the old train depot and so on.

To turn the subject to the armor would have been suspicious, so I gulped down breakfast and took off for school, saying to the Romeos, "Later."

We dozen die-hard Latin I students were silly with relief that first semester was winding down. Basketball Mike was a shadow of his formerly easygoing self, cowering behind me and chewing his fingernails, waiting for Abner's next sneak attack. Before developing a nervous condition, he'd been our star center and Magdeline High's best chance at beating rival Whitcomb. It hardly seemed fair that the entire future of Magdeline's basketball team hinged on the bony finger of a frail-looking, three-fourths blind old prune who lived on tea and crackers, and whose "Incorrrrrect!" rolled off her tongue like a death sentence. A few more of her pop quizzes and Mag High would be basketball history.

But after the initial Latin I shock in September, I'd discovered a new thing about myself. After what I'd been through—a year-and-a-half quest, the town gossiping against me, run-ins with the police, taking on Bloocifer and her babies, a futile trip to Ireland where I came eyeball to eyeball with a demon—Abner was hardly more than a minor annoyance, a fever blister on the lip of my life. I had bigger fish to fry—namely finishing what I'd started with the armor of God. Plus there was a huge social dilemma looming on the bleak winter horizon: the supremely stupid first annual masked ball.

Chapter 3

REECE and I had gotten closer since Ireland. After almost losing her over the Cliffs of Morte and that one golden moment on the Hill of Slane when I'd swear she turned into an angel for a minute, I had a hard time taking my eyes off her. It was good for my grades that we only had one class together.

But since returning from Ireland, I made a regular habit of not sitting with Reece at lunch because of Emma Stone. Reece never said anything negative about her new friend, but I knew her well enough to see she was torn. She appreciated Emma hanging around and helping with her lunch tray and books and stuff. Emma was cute and talkative and bubbly—and maybe so dense she didn't get what was going on between Reece and me. Or maybe she just didn't care. Who really knows what girls think?

Mei would always be Reece's best friend; I could see it in Reece's eyes when she read Mei's letters to me.

The guys' lunch table was full one day, so Reece waved me over. In two shakes Emma brought up the subject that I didn't want brought up. She flipped her hair and wrinkled her freckled nose at me. "Going to the masked ball, Elijah?"

Simple enough question, you'd think. But I had to weigh my words. Most guys had already staked their claims on

girls, except for Marcus who was still playing way, way cool
with Miranda Varner. I'd even seen her walking to class a few
times with square-shouldered, brown-eyed Henry Dale and
wondered what Skidmore was waiting for. I'd been hoping
to get pointers by observing a man of the world in action.
But he was no help at all. Thanks to Marcus, I was lagging
behind; the pressure to make a move built with each passing
day.

Reece was always up front about having to use crutches,
but I couldn't figure whether I should ask her to a dance
or not. Would she give me a look and say, "Hello? Earth to
Elijah. I can't dance." Or would she turn martyr and tell
me to take someone else, which was sure to start a drama I
wanted no part of. (I just plain wasn't into dancing or dressing
up like a freak and parading around in front of hundreds of
my peers.)

If I did end up going, it would be as an Indian. People
would give me grief, saying, "Where's your costume,
Creek? You wear those khakis to school!" The judges would
probably make a new award category just for me: the Dud
Award.

Why couldn't we have a regular dance like other schools?
Miss Flew, the drama director, that's why. Budget cuts in the
theater department weren't going to stop *her* from forcing
kids into costume and throwing them into a spotlight at
every opportunity. Most guys hated the whole idea, but
every last one of us got sucked into going in hopes of

winning cool stuff provided by the PTO and city council: sports equipment autographed by national players, two TVs, high-priced gift certificates, and the grand prize—a motorcycle.

Was I going? Emma's gray eyes followed my every move like a hungry coyote. Buttering a piece of bread half to death, I muttered, "I dunno."

"I hope I get asked," she said obviously. "I want to go as a flapper." She began to describe her short dress with the sparkles and fringe and little straps and how "gorgeous" it was. "Hey, Reece, if no one asks us, we'll go in a girl gang, okay?"

My ears perked. Reece poked at her food.

Emma prodded her, "You are going, aren't you?"

"It depends," Reece said, not looking up.

I ate fast and took my tray back. Retrieving my book bag from the shelf near the door, I glanced back toward Reece's table. Emma had motioned Marcus over and was gushing and pointing to Reece. Her voice cut through the cafeteria noise, and I caught the gist: she was trying to fix him up with Reece and telling him what a cute couple they'd make!

I couldn't seem to focus on any one thing for worrying about something else: Latin I exams, my social life, the dance, Mom's depression, the quest for the armor, and the demon voice. One problem muddied another. I couldn't call the Stallards for encouragement because Mom didn't want me involved with them anymore. She spent lots of time with Uncle Dorian, talking over what to do about their biological mother, Isabel, who'd been forced to give them up for adoption by a church-run workhouse in Ireland. Mom was against churches now and didn't appreciate Reece trying to keep me involved. She didn't like my calling Reece, and I felt funny myself now because of the whole masked ball thing. It seemed that the only thing Mom approved of was my hanging out with Rob in The Castle like we used to. But those days were over. She just couldn't accept the change in me.

I hardly saw Dad these days. Camp Mudjokivi was booked with winter retreats, and he had his hands full around the clock. I couldn't talk to Dom about demon stuff and risk drawing Marcus's attention. And powwows were a problem because of moms and clubs and sports moving us all on different tracks.

Marcus had been giving me strange looks, like he was trying to read me or something. When I asked him one day in study hall what he was staring at, he said, "That shabby-rugged-stud look you're going for lately—it needs work."

The thought gnawed at me that maybe he was really strategizing about Reece and me. If Miranda Varner and Henry Dale got to be a thing, Marcus would be out of luck for the dance—unless he asked Reece. He was itching for a chance to win that motorcycle, just like the rest of us guys. Things were closing in on me from all sides.

Over dinner Mom carped about the giant Santa. "Who paid for that monstrosity, Russ? If it came out of city taxes, I am going to write a strong letter! That money could be used for toys for poor children. Someone should say something to the town council!"

Dad said meekly, "From what I hear, hon, the city's planning to buy a giant snowman next year."

"Cramming Christmas down our throats with taxpayer money!" Mom snipped. She turned to me. "Elijah, how's that Latin coming? Language arts are important for college. You have to think ahead. And how many days in a row have you worn that shirt?" She passed around a bowl of instant macaroni and cheese. "Girls, you need to clean your room before bedtime. You're not babies anymore. Take some responsibility around here!"

I suddenly lost my appetite. Passing up dessert, I went to my room to stew. *Take one thing at a time,* I coached myself. *Okay, which first? The sword.* I surveyed my options and came up with one: call Francine Dowland one last time. I waited until Mom had dashed over to Uncle Dorian's about some family tree thing. The twins were in their room. Dad had rushed back to his office. The coast was clear.

I dialed the number. Francine answered, "Hello?"

"Hi. Um, this is Elijah Creek."

"Who?"

"From Magdeline, Ohio. You sent me the shoes of peace a while back."

"Oh yes. I remember. How are you?"

"I'm fine. Hey, I had a question and wondered if you could answer it."

"Well, I'll certainly try."

"We went to Ireland and visited all those castles you told us about. We even went to antique shops and asked around, but we didn't find the sword or any clue about the armor."

"That's too bad."

"I wondered if there was anything else you maybe forgot to tell us."

She paused. "I don't think so."

"I was just wondering why—with all the castles in Ireland—you all stopped at Ballymeade and Dunluce."

"I told you that Stan wanted to trace his family's roots."

"And his family once lived in those castles?"

"That's right. The MacMerrits."

I sat down on a kitchen stool and quit breathing. "Did you say *MacMerrits?*"

"That's the name."

Stan Dowland was a descendant of the bloody MacMerrits?! The ones whose tapestry at Ballymeade showed the armor of God? The ones whose victims haunted Leap Castle?! Well yeah, it made sense when I thought about it for a second. We'd followed his trail around the country and heard that name at every stop, but the whole time I'd never made the connection that *those* were the roots he was tracing.

Francine explained, "Stan read somewhere in his family's

rather unsavory history a story about hidden treasure. The story led him to buy the armor. The whole tale seemed made up to me; I didn't pay too much attention at the time. Things get hazy for me nowadays."

"I thought he bought it because it was the armor of God."

"Well, yes, he said that and even preached some sermons on it. In the end, though, it was hopes of a treasure that possessed him."

"Really. And the sword?" I asked for the umpteenth time.

"There never was a sword."

"Well, ma'am," I pressed, "if it's the armor of God, there has to be a sword."

She sighed tiredly. "That very thing drove Stan to distraction! It made him bitter, I'm sad to say."

"Did you go to Leap Castle? I'm asking because there was a story of treasure in an underground dungeon there."

"Leap Castle . . . ," she thought out loud, "not that I remember." She sounded confused.

I tried to jog her memory. "A sort of scary place in central Ireland. Off the beaten track in some lonely hills."

"No . . . I don't think so."

"'Cause the MacMerrits lived there too. It was their last stronghold before they died out."

Francine let out a hollow moan, "Ohhh . . . the end of the line. What heartache for Stan when Kate and Adam passed. Having no descendants was his bitterest pill of all."

She went on a while longer about herself and what she'd

been doing that day. I figured she was lonely, so I let her talk—keeping an ear toward the door in case Mom came back.

Finally I said, "Well, thanks for your time, ma'am. If you think of anything, call this number." I gave her Reece's phone number and told her not to talk to anyone but Reece, who'd be available most evenings. (Okay, so my motives weren't the best. But it was one possible way to have Reece start a conversation with me, which might lead to the subject of whether she really wanted to go to the masked ball.)

Mom came up to my room miffed, and I expected the worst: that she'd found out I called Francine. "I just saw your track coach at the gas station. He said you weren't sure you'd be at the postseason run on Sunday afternoon."

"I'll go," I said grudgingly.

"Then what was he talking about?"

I shrugged, tired of Mom taking all the fun out of life. "Season's over, Mom. I do plenty of running around camp to stay in shape."

"Elijah, you have to be thinking about your future. Your grades are . . . ," she strained to say, "good, but a track scholarship would help with your college fund. We're not rich, you know. Our life savings is tied up in this camp. You'll have to shoulder some of your own responsibility for college."

"That's four years away."

"Three and a half."

I sank back on my bed. "I sort of wanted to go to the lock-in at—" I couldn't call it my church without getting viped, so I just said, "with Reece's youth group."

Mom viped anyway. "An all-nighter?"

"It's safe. They have games and movies, and it's chaperoned. There's free breakfast before church. I'll be beat on Sunday afternoon after no sleep. I won't feel like running."

"Well, if you have all that time to spend, use it on something worthwhile: your schoolwork or your running. That church isn't even in town; you have friends at school. I don't understand, Elijah. You *know* how I feel about this." Practically ranting, she paused a minute and mellowed. "By the way, sweetie, I was talking to Emma Stone's mother at PTO. She says Emma speaks very highly of you."

"Yeah."

"You need to socialize more, Elijah. With other people."

I knew what she meant by "other": *other* than my clan, *other* than church people, *other* than Reece.

Mom had always tried to protect me and the twins from bad news on TV and in the papers; up to this point, I went along. My world up through middle school had been pretty much confined to Camp Mudj, school, Council Cliffs State Park, and the mundane goings on in Magdeline, Ohio.

World trekker Marcus Skidmore had said many a time that Rob and I were too sheltered. I was beginning to think he was right. So when sociology class assignments plunged into world affairs—wars, corporate corruption, government scandals, militant religions, famines, and pandemics—and when the high school Bible study class prayed about world missionaries being murdered in their cars and blown up in their churches, I sat up and took notice. I paid attention to what was happening in the Middle East where the Stallards had met the Skidmores and in Japan where Mei now lived. Marcus had relatives in northern Africa. All those places were in The Window.

I'd heard of terrible things going on around the world before, but for the first time I connected them with me. For the first time, I really truly cared.

Sometimes after Mom and Dad went to bed, I'd get up and watch the late news with the sound turned way down. Then I'd have to flush my mind of worry with a midnight B-grade horror flick. My favorite show was hosted by a middle-aged woman who was made up like a dead person and called herself Minny Kadavers. She had the best worst horror movies of all time. But after two hours of black-and-white blood and gore and the undead creeping around in my mind, I'd spin off on the real, live evil beings busting through the veil. Sometimes I'd fall asleep on the couch reading the Quella. Sometimes I'd creep up to my room and listen to night sounds until I heard Dad making coffee downstairs and knew it was morning.

One of the tackiest movies of all time was advertised for

Friday night's show: *From Hell It Came.* It was the worst.

I gathered the clan of four at my locker with a plan. "Old movie night with Minny Kadavers this Friday, one you'll love to hate. But we can't talk business or church or the Bible or the armor; it has to be goof-off time." The clan wasn't the same without Mei, and we'd pretty much lost our purpose, but they agreed semi-excitedly. As we scattered for class, I tagged along with Reece. "You can bring a friend, you being the only girl."

"Emma's probably free," she said blandly.

"Why don't you bring Miranda?" I suggested.

"We're not . . . I mean, I like her, but we don't hang out. She may not want to."

"Tell her Marcus is coming."

Chapter 4

※※

I arranged the lodge furniture around the fireplace and wheeled in a TV. Bo was around as part-time chaperone, and there'd be senior citizens on retreat wandering out of the shadows to the fridge until the wee hours—sort of like the undead. Marcus and Rob got there first. When Reece showed up with Miranda, Marcus started showing off by being Mr. Polite, getting bowls of popcorn and cans of cold pop for everyone, offering to get more wood for the fire.

We settled in for *From Hell It Came.* The scene opens on a tropical beach where an innocent guy gets executed by his island tribe for some trumped-up charge. He vows to return from Hell for revenge. The natives bury him in a tree trunk and plant him in a radioactive graveyard. The guy comes back as a tree named Tabonga with a face that's supposed to be scary but looks more like a cardboard character from a preschool play.

Rob started off being offended at the bad acting and unconvincing sets; but he soon got into the swing of it, rewriting lines as it went along and making fun of the cheap scenery and flabby natives. "Hey, natives, here comes Mr. Cranky Tree! Run—if you can!"

Tabonga toddles around through a woods that's supposed to be a jungle but looks more like West Virginia.

He chases people who run faster than him, but for some reason he always catches them. "Yeah, that's smart, people," commented Rob, "head toward the quicksand where it's safe. Oh no! Tabonga's got you! He's hugging you to death with his cardboard limbs! Oops! Into the quicksand you go!"

Rob kept us entertained with a running monologue. "Yeah, that's right, run to the edge of the cliff. Now turn and scream at the tree. There you go. Back up, a little more . . ."

In the movie the main scientist guy can't keep his mind on the deadly radioactive creature for trying to get the main scientist girl to kiss him. When she finally plants one on him, he asks, "Why'd you do that?" She says, "I don't know. My metabolism." That scene sent us off in a loony direction.

Marcus threw his arm around Miranda and said, "I'm burnin' for ya', baby, but I can't tell if it's love or calories."

"Tabonga die!" Rob cheered in a big dumb voice, mimicking the natives when they lured Tabonga into a fiery pit, raised their clubs in victory, and wandered back to what was left of the village. Hokey background music swelled, and we were supposed to think the carnage was over. Then a big hunk of smoking charcoal with eyes climbed out of the hole and toddled off to hug more natives to death.

It was the worst. We loved it.

Marcus and Miranda kidded around a lot. Rob gave the movie thumbs-up for cheesiness and hinted he might show up at the masked ball dressed as Tabonga. He tried to rope me into going as Great Oak.

"I will," I joked, "if Marcus goes as The Cedars."

Rob squealed, "Yeah! We can be a whole forest!"

We guys talked about vying for most original costume. (I was already living with the nickname Nature Boy and had no intention of parading in front of Mag High dressed as vegetation.) My real intent was to fish around for a reaction from Reece. She just picked at the popcorn in the bottom of her bowl. Miranda said she was going as Nefertiri.

Finally Marcus asked outright, "You going, Elliston?"

"It depends . . ."

On what? I wondered. *If she's able to walk? If I ask her? If Emma talks her into going with a girl gang? If she finds a costume? If I ask her and don't go as a tree?*

She gave no hints, which drove me crazy. We were already like best friends, and I didn't want to ruin that. But I also didn't want to show up as a freshman couple and be branded for life, which tends to happen in small towns. My hesitation didn't have anything to do with her disability. I just couldn't deal with any more intense feelings.

About the only thing she said to me all night was, "Elijah, are you coming down with the flu? You don't look good."

I was in the living room trying to do homework (but actually staring at a picture of Leap Castle Rob had given me and thinking how I might have to go back there to dig through that dungeon) when the phone rang.

"It's for you," Mom called. I went to the kitchen. "It's

Reece," she said darkly. "Girls shouldn't be calling boys."

My heart thumped. "We're friends," I said flatly.

Mom whispered, "If it's another one of those youth group things, you have to get that Latin grade up before test time."

I took the phone. "Reece?"

"I . . . you . . I don't know how to say this."

She sounded really upset. My gut wrenched. "What's wrong?"

"I wouldn't say it's wrong. Maybe a shock."

"What's a shock?" Was she going to the dance with Marcus?

"I don't know how to say it."

My heart sank. "Say it."

"Francine Dowland called."

My heart thumped again in a whole different direction. I wanted to ask if there was a clue, but Mom was listening from the sink. "And?"

"She remembered something."

"About . . ." I was hoping she'd say sword or treasure.

"A relative of the MacMerrit clan."

"The MacMerrits?" I asked.

Slowly Mom turned and gave me the weirdest look.

Reece said, "Okay, I'm going to give this straight, so brace yourself. Francine said that Dowland had a relative he once tried to rescue from an awful church-run home for girls. . . ." She paused.

My heart leaped into my throat. "Hold on." I covered the mouthpiece and turned to Mom. "What?"

Eerily she asked me, "How did you know that name?"

"A castle we went to . . . the people who used to own it had that name. Why?" A strange hollow in my gut and a roar in my head told me what was coming. I just couldn't believe it.

"Elijah?" Reece said from the phone.

"Hold on," I said, still looking at Mom, my mind fogging. My voice rose. "What about that name?!"

Reece answered, "It was the name of Dowland's relative."

At the same time Mom said, "It was my mother's last name."

"I'll call you back." I hung up on Reece.

My brain was in a whirl. *Hold on a minute! Crazy ol' Dowland and me—related? Through the bloody MacMerrits, who may have been the last to own the armor of God?* Chills rolled over me; a thousand questions raced through my mind. *Wait a minute! Hold on! How did we end up in the same town, his church and my camp occupying the same hill?! Did he know about this? Had he been stalking me because I was the last of his clan? Or because I had the armor?*

"How did you know that name?" Mom asked again accusingly, as if I'd breached her personal security.

I shrugged helplessly. "That last castle we visited was the MacMerrits' last stand. That's all."

She glared at me skeptically for a long moment, then slowly mellowed a little and said as if to herself, "Oh . . . I guess it's a coincidence . . . probably a common name over there." Suddenly she changed again, viping at me, her head tipped down, her eyes drilling and ready to strike. "You're not still on that armor kick, are you?"

I shrugged casually. "It's just a few more pieces, Mom. If they turn up, that'd be cool. But we're not having powwows about it. Everybody's too busy."

I retreated up to my room with my books and turned off the light. Lying in a pool of cold moonlight from my window, I took the picture of Leap Castle in my hand and studied its shape. I couldn't think straight. Not one thought lined up behind another. My mind shot across continents. *The bloody MacMerrits, a family with a chapel where a murder took place, a family who dabbled in the dark arts!* I thought about Dowland preaching the armor of God while really thirsting for treasure. I thought about Grandma Isabel trapped her whole life on the Isle of Magdeline in a church-run workhouse while I lived free in Magdeline, Ohio. My mind whirled around the gods of Mei Aizawa and her Wiccan friend Sahara versus the creator of the universe.

Mysteries of the past, mysteries of the future. The cross-shaped tomb of prehistoric Newgrange. The Day of Evil looming ahead. The shabby Blessed Assembly of the Full Gospel of the Holy Ghost and the defunct Old Pilgrim Church. A giant Santa in the center of town and angels with swords guarding The Crystal See. Words volleyed back and forth inside my skull: *saved and lost, lost and saved. Lost . . . saved. From the beginning of time until the end . . .*

pieces of the past, tragedies and truth . . . buried piece by piece.

Then and there I hatched a plan to retreat to Gilead if things got bad in the world. *Think like Dowland.* Yeah, he'd hidden his daughter and grandson in Telanoo to keep them safe. In the same way, I'd save everyone I could before the Day of Evil. I'd bring my family and my clan into Gilead. Dad and the guys and I could hunt and fish and build shelter. Mom and Reece and Reece's mom would cook and haul water and wood. Officer Taylor could come along for protection; he and Dom could stand vigil. If I kept the fires low and scouted out new hiding places, no one would find us.

All I needed was the helmet and sword. And maybe a treasure to boot, like God hinted. With a cache of money, food, weapons, ammo, we'd be safe from the evil to come.

So okay, I thought logically. *So I'm related to Dowland. So what? It might not be a bad thing in the end. Think like him and find the armor. Find the pieces of the past buried like the ones in the ground.* From the back of my closet, I dug out an old, plaid flannel shirt that I'd yanked from camp's lost and found to wear while painting. It was faded—worn out in the elbows and around the collar. I put it on and stood in front of the mirror. I studied my angled jaw and deep eyes, which looked tired, dull. The resemblance was slight, but it was there.

Think like Dowland.

I was staring in the mirror, wishing I was in Gilead or scouring the dungeons of Leap Castle, when I heard a knock at the front door and then a familiar voice. *Marcus.*

Clomp, clomp. He was coming up the steps. I threw my room together and tossed stuff under the bed.

He knocked on my door. "You in there?"

"Yeah."

He eased the door open. "Got any weapons aimed?"

"Only a couple. What's up?"

"My dad made me come." He was half serious. "You going to the dance?"

My gut went into a knot. He was here to ask permission to ask Reece. I knew it.

"I dunno."

"You should go."

And take Emma, I figured he'd say next. I'd always known from the first, since last year when Reece wanted to bring him into the group, that they had something going on. *Fine, you take Reece. I'll take Miranda,* I thought vengefully. *One night with me, and she'll never give you a second thought. I'll be so charming that I'll out-Marcus Marcus, just wait and see.*

"Reece is going," he said.

"Oh," I muttered. *Here it comes. With me, he'd say. You waited too late, chump.*

He was looking at me with that cool, cocky grin. "She'll probably want to see you there."

I looked at him. "She's going?"

"With the girl gang. She thought that'd be best."

"Oh. I didn't know . . ."

"Now you do. And there's a surprise. I think it's for you."

Oh great, I thought. *The two of you have some mystery cooked up, and I'm out of the loop.* "You going?" I asked.

"Not as a tree."

I grinned. "Me neither."

He eyed me for a moment. "You okay? You're sort of green around the gills."

"Who are you, my mother?"

"Just asking, Creek. You're gaunt. You need a haircut."

He walked out of my room, turned, and gave me an unsettled look. "Don't wear that. You look like Dowland."

I avoided everyone at school the next few days, dragged myself through classes, then ran straight home to my room. I'd stare at the picture of Leap Castle, feeling like it was calling to me. I mustered nerve for what I needed to do.

One night between frozen dinners and waiting for Mom and Dad to go to bed so I could watch TV, I took a deep breath, feeling edgy but determined. I smiled to myself. *You're getting brave in your old age, Creek.*

I took one last look at Leap Castle, the tower with no eyes; the one top center window, narrow and vertically divided like a snout; the points on the tower like horns listening, picking up only silence and wind across low-slung hills. I kept trying to make the tower into a face in my mind. I could; then I couldn't. It was; then it wasn't. I slid the picture into my pocket and went down to the kitchen. Mom stood leaning in the crook of the counter, holding a cup of tea.

I didn't know how to break it to her, so I just came out with it. "I want to go back to Ireland, to Leap Castle."

Without a hitch she said, "Absolutely not."

"You could go with me and see your mother."

"If anyone goes, it will be Dorian," she said flatly.

"I could go to navigate. I know the country now."

"No, and that settles it."

"I'll be driving soon," I half threatened.

"You can't rent a car at your age."

"Then I could bike it."

She gave me her viper stare. "Not by yourself. Not with Dorian. We can't afford the ticket."

"Aren't you ever going back to see your mom?" I asked, the edge in my voice sharper.

"I don't know."

"I think you should. And take me."

She spoke to me slow—as if I were dense. "Elijah, you have to get on with your real life."

"I'm living my real life." I turned to leave.

"Looking for some old relic is a waste of your valuable time." She sat the cup in the sink and said darkly, "You'll never find it."

I stopped and slowly turned, afraid to look her in the eye. "Wh-what . . . did you say?"

Mom eyed me vacantly, her voice flat and unfriendly. "I said you'll never find it."

Chapter 5

I ran to Dad's office. He didn't even ask what I'd come
for or wait for me to explain. "I'm really busy, son. It'll be a
couple of hours before the new folks are situated in the lodge."

"Couple hours?"

"At least. They're trickling in."

"'Kay . . . Dad, I—"

"Later," he said, not looking up from paperwork.

I practically staggered outside the lodge. I threw myself
against the wall, staring blindly down at the lake and beyond
the trees toward Gilead. *My mom just quoted a demon. I have to
get away. I'll keep my door locked. I'll put in an appearance at the
stupid masked ball, try not to make a fool of myself, figure if Reece
wants to dance and how we might do it without making a spectacle,
maybe win some cash, and then that's it. I'm out of here.*

I raided the camp's lost and found box for a costume, a
requirement to qualify for a chance at the prizes—Miss Flew's
rules. Rummaging through the box, I found an old brown
blanket, some faded beach towels, a dozen T-shirts, odd tennis
shoes, and at the bottom of the heap some pieces of leather
from an Old West tanning demonstration. *It's this or nothing.*

The night of the ball I showed up at school with my
bowie knife. I'd stopped off at the hardware store to get
it sharpened before I went into Gilead, but the store was

already closed. *Can't take a weapon into the commons, even if it looks like part of a costume. Dumb.* My outfit was a leather poncho cut open at the neck and cinched in at the waist by a belt. Other than my Indian pouch, that was the extent of my costume. I expected a reaction from Marcus, Rob, and Reece, but I didn't care.

I stashed my knife in a bush by the side door and slunk into the commons, staying to the dark periphery. The place was draped with miles of see-through gauze. White Christmas lights twinkled behind the papery veil all around, like a foggy sky full of stars. Tables circled the commons so the center could be a dance floor. The stage was dark, its curtains closed. Later on we characters would have to appear one by one on stage to be judged. I found the stag table in the corner with Justin Brill, Henry Dale, and some other guys. I took a seat, wishing I were invisible. There must have been a run on pirate hats, eye patches, and stuffed parrots at every costume department in the county—most of the guys were scraping by for a chance to win the motorcycle.

Marcus showed up as Lawrence of Arabia, suave and dashing in flowing robes and headgear. Miranda was on his arm as the queen of Egypt. When he saw me, he floated over by himself. "You made it."

"In the flesh." I looked around. He read my face.

"Not here," he half whispered.

I shot him a look.

"She will be," he said coolly.

I sat there like a knot on a log, drumming the table, half listening to the music. People were already dancing. Emma flitted around the girl gang at a table with one empty seat. She hadn't caught sight of me, thank goodness. I watched the door.

Rob came in dressed as a samurai warrior, much to my surprise. A geisha girl with a black wig and a white painted face snagged him at the door, and they found two seats near the stage. He didn't see me in the shadows of the back corner. I didn't care.

What am I doing here? This is stupid!

Miss Flew started the parade of costumes. Winners in each category were to get gift certificates. A drawing would determine who got the sports collectibles, the TVs, and the motorcycle. I went up with the stag table: four pirates, a farmer, a lab tech, a business tycoon, and myself—an Indian scout. Applause was minimal.

Lawrence of Arabia made a sweeping entrance, showing off his sand-colored robes and swirling around like a professional guy model. He waited at the bottom of the steps for Miranda, who got hoots of approval in her straight white dress with gold collar, gold sandals, cylinder-shaped headdress, and makeup just like Queen Nefertiri in the history books. They were a hit.

Several more paraded down: Elf Queen, the Masque of the Red Death, doctors and candles, wizards and butterflies and tin men. Everything from a Napoleon to a green crayon made an entrance from the closed curtains. Each character accepted what applause he got, marched down the steps, and walked back to the tables in the semidark. Then the stage was empty, the curtain black.

I slumped. Reece didn't show. She wasn't coming after all. I glared at Marcus, but he didn't look in my direction. What was this, a dirty trick? The crowd murmured. Were the judges making their decisions?

Miss Flew disappeared backstage and then reappeared a minute later, flustered and eager. "Sorry for the delay. *Ahem!* And last but not least . . . Little Soaring Eagle."

The spotlight came on. The curtains parted. She limped into the light on crutches, her blond hair and fringed dress glowing white against the black curtain. The room got quiet. Her dress was trimmed in Indian designs across the shoulders and around the bottom. Her crutches were covered with some kind of tapered strips of white material. For a minute she stood uncertainly. Then she planted her feet unsteadily, raised the crutches, and spread her arms out. I came out of my slump; my mouth dropped. The crowd gasped. Cheers and applause thundered. Her crutches were wings.

Reece didn't smile, not a big smile anyway. But a quiet confidence lit her face. Her head tipped determinedly as she extended the eagle wings for flight.

Brill leaned across the table, "Hot, Creek. Reaaaally hot."

The other guys razzed me and said things I can't repeat. Brill went on about birds of a feather, joked about the birds and the bees, and then whispered something else to the guys clumped around him. They looked at me, guffawed, and made coyote sounds. Heads turned in our direction.

Reece lowered her eagle wings and strained to see through the spotlight. She scanned the audience until her eyes stopped on me. Everyone stared at me, as if we'd had this planned all along. The guys around me stepped up their hoots and razzes.

I'd have to walk across the whole gym in my dumb scrap-leather poncho and greasy hair. Reece would be disappointed. I wanted to stand, but I couldn't. I wanted to go to the foot of the steps and escort her down, suave and cool as Marcus. But my backside seemed glued to the seat.

Uncertainly she moved to the steps. The music started. Couples got up to dance. I couldn't budge. I'd have to run to get to the steps before she came down. I'd look like an idiot. The next thing I knew, Marcus had whispered to Miranda, swept to the steps, and reached up to Reece.

My face burned. She paused, looking back at my corner confused and hurt, but finally took his hand. Over the music came an announcement about the judging, but I didn't hear it. Reece propped her wings against the stage, and Marcus led her out to the dance floor. Justin leaned over to his fellow pirate and whispered something really foul. He didn't know that I'd heard. He didn't know about the benefits of being Nature Boy, how I trained my senses to pick up sights and sounds. I got up and headed toward the back door.

I don't know what possessed me. I turned, marched back

to the guy table, and watched the stupid grins drop off their faces as I grabbed their table and flipped it—candles, drinks, snacks, and all. They went sprawling.

I ran.

I ran outside into a sudden whirl of heavy snow and grabbed the knife I'd stashed in the bushes. Wind whipped my leather wrap. Snow stung my face. I took off blindly toward home, knowing I could make it with my eyes closed if I had to. Main Street was empty. The tacky Christmas decorations, clouded by the blizzard, didn't look half bad, even sort of dreamy. But I still hated them. I hated myself, felt lower than a snail trail. *I'll get detention. How can I go back to school on Monday? How can I face Reece?* I remembered yelling at her last year during the play and how she had forgiven me then. But that was a backstage fight, not a blatant walkout in front of the whole school. I plowed through the blizzard, mortified over and over again by the fresh memory. In Reece's moment of glory, I'd left her high and dry.

My hair and jacket turned white with big flakes as I trudged through town. Camp Mudjokivi's sign had come into view when I suddenly sensed something behind me. *I'm being followed.* I pictured Justin Brill and his pirate friends coming to take me out in revenge. I whirled around, instinctively grabbing for my knife. Two blocks back—at the corner where Main Street curves to the left around the bank—I saw movement through clouds of blowing snow.

It's a truck barreling through town, taking the curve too fast, lost control . . . no, it's . . . Abner in her big white Caddy! The school sent Abner to hunt me down, and here she comes in a raging fury! She'll never see me in the blizzard. She'll run me down, and keep on trucking! Clear the decks! The huge, faint shape hit the corner of the hardware store and bounced off. The wind was howling, but I was still surprised not to hear the crash of metal.

The thing wasn't a car shape. And it was flying. Not speeding, I mean actually *airborne*—bouncing off one building, hitting the street, and bouncing off the opposite side. I heard plate glass shatter. *What in the world IS that?!* The truth dawned as it hurtled in slow motion through the blizzard—a bulky mass of red and white, a giant pair of eyes. The inflatable Santa had ripped free of its moorings and was crashing its way through Magdeline—toward me, the only pedestrian dumb enough to be out on a night like this.

Sure it was just a big balloon, but it wasn't harmless. I knew that much, having seen kids shatter femurs and crack skulls trying to control an earth ball, one fifth the size and weight of this hog-wild, goony-faced spirit of Christmas.

I wasn't sure that I could stop it and didn't care, figuring Magdeline was getting what it deserved. But my conscience spoke to me: *it could really hurt somebody, cause a wreck, take out electric lines. Power could be knocked out. Pipes would freeze and bust.* I couldn't let that happen. My hand unsnapped the strap to my bowie knife. Santa was in a high bounce. The wind caught him, slammed him into the second floor of the furniture store, and knocked him back onto the street.

Taking a knife to city property was vandalism, no two ways about that. But I couldn't let this monstrosity of a decoration ruin my town. I stepped into the street like a gunslinger at high noon, my knife hand poised behind me for maximum thrust, thinking faintly, *Mom will be proud.*

Here he comes! . . . He was on me, then over me. With more joy and less guilt than I should have felt, I drove the blade straight up into his belly and ripped hard. *Pfff!* A whoosh of air hit my face. I yanked the knife out and dashed back to the sidewalk. Santa headed out of town, slower and sloppier with each bounce. At the curve right before the camp entrance, he flopped off to the side of the road, his arms flailing, head lolling like a spent drunk.

For a moment I forgot the stupid masked ball and wished like heck that Reece, Rob, Marcus, and Mei could have been here. We'd have laughed about this for years.

I headed home, chuckling devilishly to myself, *Merry Christmas, Magdeline, Ohio.*

Rob called first thing the next morning. "What happened?"

"Whad'ya mean?" I asked sleepily.

"The chaperones were ticked at you."

"Brill and the guys said stuff, poking fun at me and Reece. I couldn't let it go."

Rob made a sound of exasperation. "Trouble."

"I'll pay for damages. I'll catch more blue racers."

He grunted again.

I said defensively, "Brill's been asking for it for a long time. He never lets up on me. What did I ever do to him?"

"It's not personal. He's like that with everybody."

"Oh yeah, what nickname did he stick on *you?*"

Long pause. When he didn't answer, I dropped the subject, having made my point. "Hey, who was the geisha girl?"

"Emily."

"Good costume. I didn't even know her."

"Yeah," Rob said with a goofy tone to his voice.

"Who won the motorcycle?"

"Greg Moline."

"Hey, uh, did Reece—"

"She left early."

"Oh." I nodded thoughtfully into the phone, sat on the couch, and stared out at the snow.

"She danced with a half dozen guys and won Most Inspiring Costume. I think the judges made up the award at the last minute just for her. Where'd you go?"

"Home."

"Well, I gotta go. I thought you should know that the chaperones were in a huddle after you left."

"Okay. Thanks."

I threw on a turtleneck and the old flannel shirt, told Mom I was going for a run, and took off for Great Oak. Last night's blizzard had left four inches of snow over the countryside. Camp was a perfect blanket of white, the lake skimmed with silver. The sky was blue, the sun warm. I filled my lungs, my feet pounding pavement until the trail ended at the dirt path we'd made into Telanoo last summer. I ran to Great Oak, suddenly weary, my eyes watery from the cold, dry air. I cleared a spot in the sunshine, faced away from the path, and plopped down against the trunk. I smelled the frozen air and felt the warm sun on my face. I closed my eyes and let my mind drift to mundane things so I wouldn't have to really think: *The snow won't last long—a day or two at the most. Then I'll work on Gilead. Gotta have a place. There's too much pressing me down. Hope Reece is okay. The snow won't last today, not if the sun stays out. I should have asked Rob about the weather. He'd know. He likes weather.*

I heard the blare of a distant train, the wind swaying the upper branches of Great Oak, and dead leaves somersaulting past me on the ground. Facing east, I was sheltered from the wind. The buzz of the golf cart approached through the woods from the direction of the camp. *Bo's checking the path. It won't need clearing. The snow'll melt by late afternoon. Dad'll want me to do the nature talk for the Whitcomb Nature Club's winter hike. That'd be good—a perfect day for the old folks. Crisp and clean. I need to be out and about.* I listened as the cart kept coming—past where the paved path ended a few yards behind me. The engine stopped. *Rats. Bo spotted me; he must need work done now. I'm not in the mood. I'm tired.*

A small voice cut across the quiet. "I thought you were Stan Dowland sitting there."

Reece!

Chapter 6

I shot to my feet so fast that my head swam. I spun around. There she sat behind the steering wheel of the cart.

"Hey," I said lamely.

In a peacoat and jeans, her face pink from the cold, she stared at me a long time. I wondered if she'd stolen the key from the maintenance shed or gotten permission from Bo. *Had Mom told her I was here, or did she just know? Am I even awake? Or is this a nightmare, the spirit of bad Christmas parties past coming to chew me out?*

She snorted. "Faded flannel, all scraggly looking—some clan leader you are."

"What clan? The Nowhere Fast clan?" The bitter edge in my voice startled me.

"Oh, grouchy and mean too. That's just super!" she snipped.

She got out of the cart with the help of her de-feathered crutches. Her eyes never left me. "Everyone cheered me but you. *Everyone* clapped and said what a cool costume it was. Marcus danced with me—and Rob and a half dozen other guys—to show me I don't always have to be a freak; to say, 'Hey Reece, you can be like the other girls for one night.'"

"You're not a freak," I said, my mind chanting, *Don't mess it up, don't mess it up.*

"Everyone but *you.*" Seething, she came right up to me and backed me into Great Oak, her eyes narrowing. "You owe me, Elijah Creek."

"Everyone in the gym was staring at me," I explained. Lousy excuse and I knew it. *Don't mess it up! Think!*

She shot back, "They were staring, all right. Staring at the huge gap between where I was standing and where you were sitting there with your . . . your pirate buddies."

"They're not my buddies!" I shot back. "They're jerks."

I wasn't about to mention the stuff they were saying about her—about us. Not now, not ever.

She agreed nastily. "Yeah. Jerks who couldn't get dates because they were too scared and too full of themselves to get out on a dance floor and move around for five minutes with someone who'd been hoping and praying for weeks she'd get to come."

It took every ounce of willpower to stay put. Part of me wanted to turn tail and run into Telanoo where she couldn't get at me, and part of me wanted to grab her and grovel and say how sorry I was. My mind was a mess.

She interrupted my thoughts. "I want to climb Great Oak."

I looked down at her hard-set face. She was serious.

"That's not a good idea," I replied.

She didn't flinch. "You said you can see everything from up there; you told me that once. That's what I want to see: everything. You owe me."

"I don't want to be responsible for you dying," I said bluntly.

"If you don't help me, I'll try it myself. Then you *will* be responsible."

Reece wasn't going to budge. But maybe I could put her off until she settled down and got some sense. "Well, uh . . . okay. When it warms up—"

"I want to go now. Pay up."

I objected, "Reece . . ."

"Now!" Her mouth was set, her eyes drilling into me.

"Without me you can't get up to the first branch," I argued.

"Just watch me. I'll use my crutches as a ladder."

"You'll kill yourself."

"And it'll be your fault. I brought rope to pull myself up."

"You'll hang yourself."

"Your fault." She repeated it matter-of-factly and went back to the cart to retrieve a length of heavy rope.

I followed her, throwing out any excuse to make her stop. "What about your mom? Does she know what you're doing?"

"She knows." Reece pushed me out of the way with her crutch and went back to Great Oak. "Mom knows how much you hurt me, and she wasn't about to say, 'No, sweetie, you just stay on the ground; stay in the background and be a big nobody. Be a cripple; don't do what everyone else does.' She wants me to stretch my limits." Reece unwound the rope and shot me an angry look. "So I'm climbing a tree."

I studied the chinquapin oak, the biggest, tallest tree in Owl Woods. Instinctively I started evaluating the shortest gaps between branches, the easiest, safest way up.

"My arms are strong," she said with a kind of nervous anger. "If you help me get to the first branch, I can pull myself up to the next."

"Okay," I said helplessly. I made a stirrup with my hands and hoisted her up. She sat down hard and grimaced.

"Reece . . ." But I couldn't tell her that she couldn't climb. Not after last night.

"Okay, wait," she said, thinking. "Okay, you climb up and pull me up until my feet find a branch. That'd be the easiest."

"Shouldn't I be beside you in case you start to fall?"

"I'll hold on."

I climbed to the limb above her and looked down at her blond hair whipping in the wintry breeze, feeling the chill through my shabby shirt. "It's much colder at the top with the wind and all." I knew how the cold affected her.

"Good," she said sarcastically. "I like wind; it's refreshing."

I'd climb one branch above, she'd let go of her branch and grab onto my arms, I'd pull her up and talk her onto the next limb: "move your foot left," "go right," and so on. She didn't weigh much, but the strain of having her life in my hands wore me down. By the time we were halfway up Great Oak, she was trembling from the cold and the pain. I was unsteady myself. Sure, I helped Nori and Stacy climb trees all the time . . . campers too, but never Reece, never to the top of Great Oak in Telanoo. No one had climbed it but Rob and me. "Let's stop and rest. Hey, look how you can see the lodge from here!" I said, hoping she'd be content with this view of the camp.

She kept her eyes on the swaying top of Great Oak and gulped hard. "I'm climbing . . . to there."

"But from here you can see—"

"Keep going!"

By two-thirds of the way up, her fingers had gone numb, and she was shaking all over. The wind was swaying the narrow trunk—I was truly scared. My fingers were purple; my ears burned. "Hey, Reece," I laughed weakly, "we'll probably get stuck up here like two house cats, and the fire department will have to come get us down."

Concentrating on one hand and then the other, she hauled herself higher and didn't crack a smile. I don't think she even heard me.

I dropped down so we'd be eye to eye. "Listen to me!" I yelled over the wind. "This is too dangerous. I wouldn't come this high by myself, not in winter in high wind. Your fingers can't hang on. The branches are brittle with cold."

"Then you go back down, coward."

"Come on, Reece!"

"Coward!" she blurted again. Her blue eyes filled with tears that ran down her face. "You can climb trees to the top, explore Telanoo, face down Dowland, and pull me back from the Cliffs of Morte, but you couldn't take thirty measly steps for one moment to make me feel normal?" A hiccup caught in her throat. "All the work my mom did on my costume and—" she broke into sobs, "and you couldn't take a few crummy steps! Who's disabled now, Elijah? Who's the *real* cripple?"

Angrily, Reece wiped her eyes and reached for another branch. "A few more feet to the very top. I'm going!"

I didn't know what else to say. I'm not a man of words. So I kissed her.

She reeled back, shocked. "What'd you do that for!?"

I was confused. I thought girls who liked you *wanted* you to kiss them.

She raged at me. "Elijah, in front of the whole school, you act like I don't exist, but then when we're up here in the middle of nowhere, you . . . you . . ." I was bracing for a slug in the nose, gearing up to dodge her fist, and planning how to keep her from losing her grip on the branch and plunging us both down the full height of Great Oak, when she kissed me back. "Coward!" she said the third time. Then she hugged me hard like it didn't matter what I'd done.

Girls make no sense.

Reece wedged her foot into the next crook, pulling herself up. "Why didn't you dance with me?"

Nothing I could do would get me off the hook. "I . . . I . . . ," I stammered. There was no excuse. "It . . . it was my metabolism," I joked lamely.

Her head dropped, and she broke into a giggle. Then she

cried a little more and slugged me with her fist and said, "Tabonga will die."

We made it to the top of Great Oak without another word. It was as if we'd said everything we needed to with the word *coward,* two kisses, and a couple of slugs. "Look down," I said. Our eyes followed the trunk of Great Oak to where the golf cart sat, small as a toy. Reece clung to me for dear life. "Amazing, huh?" I said it so proudly you'd have thought I had something to do with the tree and the view. "Not as high as the Cliffs of Morte, but the greatest view around here."

She locked eyes with me, tears sparkling on her eyelashes. "I've wanted to be up here . . . with you . . . forever!"

"Me too," I said, and then added, "I mean, I didn't think it would ever happen. But I'm glad too. Hang on. Don't get distracted and let go."

In all directions—Camp Mudj, Telanoo, Council Cliffs, Morgan's farm, Magdeline—I pointed out landmarks, even the direction of her apartment. For me it was like seeing my world for the first time.

Reece kept looking around and around like she was trying to memorize every detail. "I feel like I could really fly. Oh, Elijah, do you see how it works out? If you hadn't ignored me, I wouldn't have gotten mad, and I wouldn't be here. He always works it out. Always. I wouldn't trade this for anything."

We wrapped our arms around the thin trunk and each

other, shivering and swaying in the biting wind. The branches clicked and crackled, making an unnerving sound. Reece couldn't have cared less.

There I stood at the summit of my own private kingdom, Reece with me—really with me. Feelings welled up, and it seemed that anything was possible now. We were perched up here like eagles, unafraid and free. I'd found myself again; I knew who I was and what I wanted from life. I had God and Reece. When Mom was her old self again, the clan could restart the quest. And come spring, I might even get semi-famous in track if I trained well. Reece was like my good-luck charm. Life was okay again.

There's nothing like standing at the top of a tall, tall tree and looking around at your life. You really can see everything.

By the time we got back to the foot of Great Oak, Reece was having trouble. She tried to pretend that she was okay, but I knew better. She looked up bravely, "I knew it wouldn't be easy. Give me a day to rest; I'll be fine."

"Are you sure?"

"Hey, it's just a little pain."

I'd hoped we could go sit under the natural evergreen tent of The Cedars, out of the snow, but she needed to get to the lodge and rest before her mom picked her up. I drove us to the front door as some adult group was heading in for a meeting. "It's busy. We'll have to go back to the house. You can call your mom from there."

We were settled on the couch with hot chocolate when Mom burst though the front door, mad as a hornet. She took one look at Reece and turned to me with an accusing frown. "Elijah, where have you been? It's been hours!"

I stood. "Hi, Mom, I went for a run like I said." I made a code face to say I had company and could she please tone it down. "But Reece came over—"

Mom didn't get the code. "Officer Taylor called about last night. What were you thinking!?"

Officer Taylor? The school called the police over a dumb table!? It was only because Reece was there that I stayed calm. "I'm sorry, Mom, but it was not a huge deal. I can't believe they called the cops. Those guys were acting like—"

As if she didn't hear me, she went on, "If this is supposed to be some kind of favor to me, it's rather twisted. We're going to have to pay for all that damage!"

"What damage? It's a lousy table!"

She counted off on her fingers, "You break the table with that little tantrum at school, then you go through town on a rampage and slash the Santa—sure I hated the thing too, but you don't destroy public property—then you knock over trash cans and break store windows like a common vandal! *What has gotten into you?!*"

"No . . . no, Mom . . . hold on."

"I will not hold on! Your dad's on his way, as if he needs this aggravation! Don't you move an inch!"

I was hoping Reece's mom would pick her up before Dad

came, to save me more mortification, but no such luck. The twins were sent to their room—where they were probably hearing every word from the heat duct.

It was embarrassing trying to explain to my parents how I'd acted about Reece at the ball, how Brill's gang had stepped over the line, how I'd messed up being a gentleman but couldn't let guys talk bad about girls, especially Reece. I did the best I could to explain. Throwing the table was an afterthought, I said, because there were more of them than me, and it was my way of making a statement. But saying the whole thing out loud made me sound like a coward *and* an idiot. "I wasn't thinking about what people would think."

There was a glint of approval in Dad's eyes when I said the part about being a gentleman, but Mom said, "It doesn't sound to me like you were thinking at all!"

Officer Taylor came over as Reece's mom showed up. We all gathered in the living room and put me on trial. I told them what really happened in town. I even suggested that Officer Taylor check the ropes that held the Santa. "See if they've been cut or if they tore loose." I showed him the murder weapon I'd used on Santa to protect the town.

Mom shrieked, "You took a knife to school?!"

I backtracked to explain the knife—Mom shaking her head the whole time—then I went on.

"I saw the windows break—it was Santa, not me. Look around at the scene on Main Street; you won't find a rock or stick or anything used to break windows. It wasn't me. I'll swear it on a Bible if you want me to."

Mom rolled her eyes.

Officer Taylor shook his head. "Not necessary. A man's as good as his word." He wrote some things in his notebook.

Dad said, "Darrell, this isn't like our son; you know that. He's gotten himself into some unusual situations lately, but he doesn't flagrantly destroy public property. He's a good boy."

Taking a cue from Dad, Mom said, "He is a good boy. Elijah's usually very responsible. This incident is the result of too much stress in his life. He needs to cut back on his involvements—" Her eyes skimmed over Reece and landed squarely on me, "which I've been trying to tell him."

Reece's head tipped forward; her hair hid her face.

When Officer Taylor asked a few more details and seemed satisfied, I walked him to the door. He glanced over my shoulder, saw my parents talking in the kitchen, and said in a near whisper, his kind eyes resting solidly on me, "Rachel and Reece—they're strong."

"I know."

He tapped me on the shoulder with his knuckle. "You take care of yourself. Looking a little thin there; eat your meat and potatoes. Runners need protein. I'll file this report and see if we can confirm your story. Depending on what we find, we may want you to come in for further questioning."

Reece's mom helped her to the door. On her way out,

Reece slipped a note into my hand. "I brought this last night, but I didn't get the chance to give it to you." She smiled at me as if all was forgiven. "A poem from English class. I thought of you when I read it." I slipped it into my pocket.

That night after dinner, when Dad had gone back to work, Mom grilled me about what Reece and I had been doing in the woods. I slumped on the couch while she rattled dishes in the sink, interrogating me. "Why did she follow you all the way back there in the first place? When she came by and asked where you were, I had no idea she'd follow you, for goodness sake! And why Bo gave her permission to drive the cart, I'll never know. Whose idea was that? It's not policy to let the disabled drive themselves."

I came out of my slump. "She's my friend, Mom. I'm allowed to have friends. Lay off Reece."

She marched over and glared down at me. "Don't you use that tone with me! You're allowed friends. Of course. Don't be silly. But bad influences, no. Absolutely not. Being a church girl doesn't make Reece a good influence," she said acidly. "I'm not naïve."

"You've got to be kidding me!" I jumped to my feet. "Reece a bad influence? That's insane!"

"How dare you call me insane!!" Mom screamed.

I hadn't thought that she'd take it personally. But I guess

with her just finding her biological mother in a home for the aged, with her mind being pretty much gone, it hit Mom the wrong way. I hadn't meant it like that, but before I could apologize, she said, "When your father comes in, we're discussing your increasingly rebellious behavior. Until then, go to your room, Elijah!"

I stormed up the stairs and muttered under my breath, "I'll go farther than that."

Chapter 7

AT 11:00 Dad was still out. I'd already begun to quietly pack my gear: tent, sleeping bag, bow and arrows, fire kit, leather poncho. Mentally I made a list of tools from the maintenance building I'd need: shovel, ax, rope, hammer, nails, lantern. My heart was beating hard. I hoped Mom wouldn't come in, but I was prepared: I had books spread on the desk as if I were in the middle of studying for tests. My closet door was open and ready in case I needed to hide the gear.

I felt bad sneaking around behind her back. But I'd had it. Something was working on her against my Christian life—and against the quest—plain as day.

I started a short list of food I'd eventually need: energy bars, canned meat, trail mix.

None of us had talked to the Stallards for a while, but they needed to know we hadn't given up. They were probably lying low because of potential antiquities hounds like Cravens. Reece could send a quick note saying that the quest continues. I dug out their address and jotted it down to give to her at school on Monday.

For weeks a picture had been forming in my mind: a stone hut built against the gorge wall of Gilead. A roof of sticks covered with plastic and camouflaged with forest debris, a canvas flap for a door. I'd take a day here or there to work on it, the same way I had with the road. With a little ingenuity and a few weeks of elbow grease, I could make a base camp.

From there I'd be free to sweep Telanoo for the last of the treasure. We'd have a place—a clan hideout where no one could find us—to stash the whole armor of God if Mom or anyone else got too hostile over it. It'd be a bigger surprise for Rob, Reece, and Marcus than my road through Telanoo. If and when the Day of Evil came, we'd all have a place to hide.

I'd load my stuff at first light on Sunday, drive it out to Telanoo as far as my road went, then haul it the rest of the way and have the cart back before anyone else was up. I'd finish chores and tell Dad I needed to be by myself. He'd understand. Mom would be glad I wasn't going to church. Then I'd get to work.

Part of me wanted to disappear altogether. I hated the prospect of facing the police again, of going to school, of owning up to the masked ball committee and Miss Flew about making a big scene. I was tired of Latin homework, monster Christmas decorations, and dumb dances designed to make guys feel like losers. I was fed up with Emma's peskiness but didn't want to be the reason for the end of Reece's friendship with her. I'd spent all my snake money to get to Ireland, and for what? A depressed mom who greeted me from behind her dark cloud every time I came home from church, stealing away the good feelings I'd worked up there. Home had meant something, but with Mom so gloomy all the time and the twins getting clingy and wild, that was crumbling too.

My high-flying feelings from the top of Great Oak had disappeared like a puff of smoke. *Too much stuff rattling around in my head! I need space. I want El-Telan-Yah to tell me where the sword is. He will. He's gotten me this far. I'll find out what I need to know in Gilead.* I got my clothes ready and threw on the only clean shirt I had—the white one I wore the day I was baptized.

For all its isolation and strangeness, I loved Gilead: an unnaturally deep crack in a high ridge—water-formed for sure. I recalled Reece's global flood theory and decided that might be the best explanation. My hiding place was near the end of the gorge. The rim was so overgrown that at its narrowest you could plow through a thicket and drop right into oblivion. I surveyed my hideout with satisfaction. *One day soon I'll bring the Stallards back here and show them the stone scratchings. We'll keep the discovery to ourselves, at least until we've found all of the armor of God.*

I stashed my gear in a dry spot under the ledge, breathed in cold, still air. I listened to the trickle of water from above which made a straight, tiny stream through the gorge. *This is home,* I told myself with secret satisfaction: *Gilead,* "rocky place" according to the Quella footnotes.

I skimmed the gorge for resources to build my hut. The first wall would be the side of the cliff itself, the straightest rise being several yards away from the trickle. In the other direction—toward the mouth of the gorge—lay a slab of stone five or six feet long and three feet across, slanting up a dirt bank. The stone was huge, but if I dug around it and dislodged it from the dirt, I'd be able to push it down the hill—maybe. I could shove a log under it and roll it into position. I might need the guys to help me fit it into place. But maybe not . . . I spotted a nice smooth sapling right away. That'd be my rolling log.

With a lot of maneuvering and sweat, I could scoot it down to the floor of the gorge, fit it into a shallow trench perpendicular to the cliff, and brace it with smaller stones. It would be my second wall. I'd pile up stones from the stream to make a third wall and then construct a roof of plastic and forest debris. A canvas flap would make a fourth wall of the house in Gilead.

Planning ahead, I piled rocks on the hard dirt canyon floor in the path of the slab, in case it got away from me. If it hit the ground flat, I'd never get it upright. For an hour I gathered stones from the creek and piled them at the foot of the embankment to catch the slab.

Sweating in the sunny, windless cold, I ditched my poncho and knife and dug around the slab, wishing for better tools: a pointed shovel, even a trowel. I hadn't thought about a trowel. A flat creek stone would have to do.

Once I'd dug a considerable pile of dirt out from under the slab, I positioned my back against the trunk of a tree up the slope, braced my feet against it, and pushed. It hardly budged. "You're heavier than I thought."

I took a break, got a drink of water from my canteen, and cut down that sapling, lopping off the top and stripping the branches until it was smooth enough for rolling.

After a snack I dug further under the edge of the slab with the stone trowel. "You're not spoiling my plans, rock," I huffed. "I *will* have a shelter in Gilead: one cliff wall, one slab wall, one creek stone wall, and a slanted roof so rain won't puddle. I doubt rain will reach the roof. We're pretty far under the ledge. That's how it is in my head," I said to the rock. "You're part of my plan."

For another hour I worked it down the hill inch by inch, pushing with my legs until my thighs and back ached. It had to be below freezing—the snow still lying in shady patches—but sweat ran from my forehead and down my back. After several hours I'd edged the slab to where the slope of the hill fell away five feet above the gorge floor. A third of the slab hung over. One more solid heave and it would go. It hadn't moved exactly the way I wanted, so I repositioned the pile of stones beneath it. *If I'm gonna get this baby upright to make my wall, I can't let it land flat. Can't.* Studying some more, I calculated how it might fall on the stones, how I'd work a log under it, roll it into position. *Yeah, I'll definitely need the guys to set it safely and firmly in place.*

That part has to be done just right. I grinned. Wouldn't want to wake up in my hut with you on my chest, big fella.

I thought about Newgrange, Ireland's prehistoric tomb, and wondered how they did it—its ring of megaliths hauled from miles away, the passageway lined with standing stones. Dr. Eloise was probably right: the ancient people were superhumans.

Back up the slope, I positioned myself one last time against a tree and braced for one final push. *Heave-HO! Breathe. Again! Little farther . . .* It tottered; the bank crumbled under it on one side, and the slab started sliding away from my pile of stones. *Uh-oh.*

I jumped down, got underneath it, and raised my shoulders, hoping to tip it back toward the stones. *Push, push! To the stones!* I thrust myself back. But the slab's incredible weight suddenly bore down on me. *Coming down!* Was it in place over the stones? My knees wobbled; I groaned. *Not giving up! This close. One more heave, one more . . .* I felt my shinbones bowing under the pressure. Fear shot through me. *Breaking! Get out! Go!* Pressed down into a crouch I threw myself forward. *Move!* The slab scraped my backside and hit the back of my thigh. I tried to lunge forward. Down I went, landing on my knee and forearm. *Go, go, man!* I heard the grind of rock against rock, slab crushing stones, and my own primal cry as I desperately pulled myself forward, the slap of my belly hitting the ground.

In the blink of an eye everything had changed. The weight of the slab had nearly flattened my pile of stones, trapping my left foot in the rubble. I couldn't move, but I wasn't worried. I wiggled my toes. There was pressure on my foot from all sides, but it didn't really hurt. Awkwardly—because I was pinned facedown—I turned to evaluate my situation. The slab was frighteningly large from this angle, bigger and thicker than it had seemed before, now sandwiching me to the ground. I gave my foot a yank. No luck. *I'll have to wriggle my foot out of my shoe to free it,* I thought calmly, though I knew how tight the laces were. My foot was much bigger than my ankle. How could I work it through that small opening? I yanked harder. The sound of stone grinding on stone stopped me. The pressure on my ankle tightened. *Hold it. Stop and think.* Propping on my elbows, I looked back again. The slab was at such an angle that I couldn't see under it. It was poised to slide if provoked, to crush my thigh, then hip, all of me if it slid far enough. I wondered if the stones surrounding my foot were cracking under the weight. If I yanked too hard, would they crumble? *Careful. Careful.*

I lay my face on the cold dirt and rested. *Don't panic. You can get out of this. You will. They'll find you.*

I lay there for a long while not thinking, just listening to myself breathe. What a wonderful sound, breathing. I ignored the trickle of water. I couldn't think about water. Then I realized what time of day it was. The sun had gone behind the rim, the sky was rosy. Darkness would come quickly.

A terrible dread settled on me. I'd never planned for this. I couldn't reach anything: food, water, my sleeping bag, wood. Dad always taught in survival classes, "Shelter is first priority, especially on a cold night." But I wasn't thinking about shelter. I was thinking about fire.

No cedar branches to make a bed. Only cold, hard dirt. I remembered how Marcus and I had banked sand around Reece that night she went down on the Hermits' Cave trail, how I'd brought water for her to drink and talked to her to keep her spirits up until help came. I had none of that here. But what worried me was a winter night without fire.

"If it rains or snows and you can't find dry wood, you might have to endure a night without fire," Dad told survival campers, "but crawling up under a spruce tree makes great shelter."

The closest tree was leafless and seventy feet away.

"On frigid nights make a debris shelter of boughs and leaves and then burrow in."

I had nothing to burrow under. Even stretching my arm to its full extension, I still lacked a foot in reaching the cord of my sleeping bag.

"Keep your core warm, whatever you do," Dad would warn his students. "Frostbitten fingers are one thing. Hypothermia's another."

The cold ground was already leeching the warmth from my chest. I couldn't think about my foot or water or food until I had that sleeping bag. With a sharp stab of reality, I understood that this situation was not in survival manuals. The twelve inches between the sleeping bag cord and me was the distance between life and death.

A tool. I need a tool. A stick . . . my knife! I twisted around to see where I'd left it. It lay not far from my free foot. With the toe of my shoe, I edged it up in an arc toward me, careful not to jar the other foot. *Easy, easy, drag it, not too big an arc. Keep it within reach. Careful, careful.*

Got it! Twenty minutes until complete darkness. Once night fell, I wouldn't be able to see the cord. *Get the bag, then worry about everything else. You can do it,* I encouraged myself. I reached the tip of the knife toward the bag. *Don't cut the cord, pull it toward you . . . easy, easy. Drat!* It rolled from under the blade and sprang back. I slapped the ground and cursed. Then I dropped my head on my arm and rested a minute. *You cannot panic!* Concerned that I'd get too anxious and cut the cord, I turned the handle out and grasped the blade, concentrating every muscle on reaching the cord while I could still see it. Stretching until I trembled from the strain, holding my breath for control, I touched the cord with the tip of the knife handle. Steadily the knife handle pressed and pulled on the cord until it was within my reach. I grabbed the cord with a bloody hand, not realizing until then that I'd sliced my finger. I yanked the bag over to me and pressed my face into it like a kid to his favorite teddy bear. I breathed it in. Quickly, forcing myself to stay calm, I unrolled it. By the time I'd worked the sleeping bag under and around me, it was dark.

I worried a little that my smells—especially the blood—would attract coyotes.

I had matches and a piece of paper in my pocket—Reece's poem—but nothing else to burn except for my clothes and a few stray leaves. I could stay awake to listen for leaves to blow past and collect them. *Wouldn't be worth it. Save your energy. You might need it later.*

Later . . . The word echoed in my mind. I worked my ankle and my toes—overjoyed that I felt them. I tested my foot's range of motion; it was encased without an inch to spare in any direction. But no crushing pressure.

Later. How much later?

Until someone comes.

I lay awake fighting cold and panic. If only I'd broken my leg free of the rock! I could've made a fire, got water, food, made a splint, and limped home. I looked longingly through the darkness to where my pack was, tossed in a recess in the cliff wall not far from the ancient scrawls which read "the hand of God is a shield—a prayer." I'd tossed everything—medical kit, plastic garbage bags for a dry bed, canteen—in a pile so it would be safe.

As I weighed my options, horror crept into my belly . . . into my bones. I could not have been in a worse situation.

Okay, look at the advantages. Find something good here. A survival camp should be protected from the wind; that's one thing. I'm tucked under a cliff; that's another. The gorge has a southeast/

northwest orientation, southeast being the open end. I'll get morning sun. Good. And I'm strong. I can take extremes in temperature—I wade barefoot in winter. People will look for me. Mom and Dad. Reece and Rob and Marcus. They won't give up.

Facts came rushing past. I'd just told Dad that I had to get away. I didn't say where or for how long. Mom knew I wanted to go back to Ireland. But my toothbrush was still at the house. My suitcase. My passport. I pictured my bedroom as I'd left it. What clues would they find? Open books. The note on my desk with Stallards' address. A list of food. They'd think I was hitchhiking to Chicago! Would my mom call the police on the Stallards? *By morning, there'll be a manhunt for me around town. Then they'll sweep wider. The Stallards will be in the papers. Their picture . . . and mine. My picture! What if Cravens or one of his cronies sees it and tracks down the armor? What if days go by while everyone blames the Stallards?*

What if weeks go by?

They might search Telanoo, but not here. They'll follow the road to Devil's Cranium and check the ruin. They'll scour Council Cliffs. But I'm not there. I'm here! No one knows I'm here. No one but . . .

"El-Telan-Yah?" I called into the cold, eerie darkness. "You know I'm here. Send someone!"

Chapter 8

WATER source. At first light after an awful night, I twisted my neck to look up to the overhanging cliff. A small section glistened with groundwater. I listened for drips. It had been a dry winter so far. I worried about my foot and told my brain to work my toes to keep the circulation going. I couldn't feel them.

Rearranging the sleeping bag around me, I thought about Camp Mudj. I'd have given anything to be there: the lodge floor, a back cabin, a tree house. I wouldn't need my warm bed or one of the dinners Mom used to make. I wouldn't need the sound of the twins running through the house or the smell of Dad's coffee wafting up the steps in the morning. Yeah, a bunk with a one of those raggedy brown blankets would be great. A peanut butter sandwich would be a feast. I'd never complain again. I wouldn't, not once I was back home.

I lay there listening to my own breathing for a long time.

Listen, God, you see the mess I'm in. Can't you just flip this stone off me? Send an angel like you did at Jesus' tomb, and give it a big heave-ho. Remembering Reece's prayer when she went down in Hermits' Cave, I thanked God ahead of time for whatever he wanted to do for me. He knew where I was. In one way that thought helped. In another way it was terrifying beyond words.

I didn't want to replay the minute the slab had fallen, how things might have been different if I'd moved a split second faster. *It happened the way it happened. Can't change the past. Only the future.* A knot of dread and gnawing hunger filled my gut. *Only the future.*

If I'd broken a leg, I'd have been able to crawl and could have found small animal trails, or built a snare. I'd never dressed and cooked a rabbit or anything, but . . .

Why are you thinking about how to fix food? about how to trap an animal when you can't even move your foot? Idiot. You're the trapped one.

I know.

As the day brightened, I thought about Reece, how she'd been in traction for weeks over the summer, how she must have felt trapped.

Cold. I think my toes are still moving. Thirsty. Water is more important than food. I'll need water soon. They'll come. Someone will come.

When—February? April?

I could live a week or more without water in decent conditions—but on my belly on hard cold ground, immobile? I thought about my knife, a critical tool for surviving, for cutting kindling and rope, for hacking boughs for shelter . . .

I thought about my foot.

It's the only thing stopping you from getting out of here.

I know.

So?

So I'm not ready to part with it yet, God.

What was he telling me? I thought of other ways: I could start yanking and keep yanking until I broke every bone in my foot and pulled the bloody stump through the hole. Then I'd drag myself to the tree, make a fire, and hope that some doctor somewhere would know how to rebuild a foot from a pile of splintered bones.

The foot may already be dead. You don't know.

No, God, I don't know! I answered angrily.

I suddenly rose up on my elbows, startled. *The tone. The tone in his voice.* I replayed it in my mind. He didn't sound the same. Of all the times I'd heard him speak before, he'd always sounded strong—powerful but quiet. And of all the things he'd said, I'd always had a feeling, a *knowing* that he cared—that he loved me. He never sounded teasing, taunting, like Justin Brill on his worst day. He had never called me an idiot. Chills rolled over me.

You're not him!

Silence. He'd slipped away.

Shadows moved as the sun tracked across the sky, its warmth settling on my back. *Fire is everything.* I fingered the knife, thought about my options, and blocked every voice speaking to my spirit. Random, disconnected thoughts floated through my brain. *I never found the helmet or the sword.* I ached with regret. *If they don't find me in time, if . . . if I'm gone, will the others give up the quest?*

I envisioned them finding my body gnawed by coyotes and bears, pecked by birds. I saw myself like Salem was when we'd found him at the ruin: stinking, eyes shrunken, covered with maggots. I saw the rescue squad bringing me out in a body bag. I saw Mom sobbing, clinging to Dad. I pictured Dad looking out over the hills, his jaw clenched as he watched the coroner drive away.

Blinking back tears, I imagined my funeral. Reece would be there. She'd rush up to my closed coffin and drape herself over me sobbing—no . . . no, she wouldn't. She'd stand there like a soldier, comforting everyone as they passed by, saying, "We know where he is," and lift her teary, smiling eyes heavenward. She'd probably start dating Justin Brill and bring him under her influence, changing his life like she'd changed mine. Reece would go on without me. She'd be fine.

I sniffled, remembered where I was—still alive for now. *Cut the drama, Creek. Save your brain cells for survival.*

I remembered the Quella. Where was it? I'd stuck it in the folds of my sleeping bag at the last minute. It must have gotten tossed aside when I flung open the bag. I looked around and there it was, almost under me. I grabbed it, turned it on eagerly, and scrolled down randomly, wondering who was behind my predicament: God or Satan.

I didn't know. My foot was encased but not crushed. Had to be more than coincidence that it had slipped into a foot-shaped space in the rubble. I took great comfort in that. Where do I start? *Rock.* I looked it up. The first reference was about the Rock of Israel who blesses people with the heavens above and from the deep that lies below.

I read from the *Warrior:* "The LORD is my rock, my fortress and my deliverer; my God is my rock, in whom I take refuge. He is my shield."

In one story people were thirsty, and Moses struck a rock and water came gushing out. Welling up with hope, I felt around for a stone. *If I hit the cliff, would I get water?* I found only one stone, and it was too big to hurl. It didn't seem like there were any messages in the Quella for me.

The hours wore on. The sun moved. I got up on my knees to stretch but could only get into a low lunge position because of the slab hovering over my thigh. I fought my mind against replaying it over and over, how I'd waited a third of a second too long. I lay there eyeing my backpack where there was food but no way to get to it. I scratched in the dirt with my knife, wondering if I should leave a message . . . in case.

Don't dull the knife. You might need it. . . .

I shuddered. How would I do it? I could barely reach to my calf, much less apply a tourniquet. *That's a lot of muscle to cut through. And the nerves!* I'd probably pass out from the pain and bleed to death. *I could take it off at the knee. What good is any part of a leg without a foot anyway? I'll need a tourniquet. My belt.* I worked it out of the belt loops and poked holes, starting at about eight inches from the buckle and every inch after that. When I was ready, I'd tighten it around my leg, then tighter and tighter until all feeling was gone.

Thirst had settled in. *Get used to it,* I thought dully.

Through the day I'd call out every few minutes, "Hey! Help! I'm down here!!" No one could hear me. I knew that. I felt lonelier because of the silence that followed my yells. So I quit.

The day wore on. I tried pulling my leg every few minutes, kept telling my brain to move my foot. *Send blood to it. Keep it going.*

Mid-afternoon, I began to feel different. It's hard to describe. A kind of inner warmth and comfort settled over me, sort of like after eating a big meal. My belly screamed for food, but the comfort went through my whole body in spite of the hunger. I lay there for hours just thinking about the comfort. Nothing changed, but I wasn't as afraid.

As the sunlight turned amber, I screamed for help for a while, and then went back to the Quella. I read about Elijah all through the Bible. The first Elijah from twenty-eight hundred years ago lived a pretty crazy life before he was sucked up into a tornado. John the Baptist was called the second Elijah, a voice crying in the wilderness. Then the commentary said that at the end of time, two witnesses appear on the scene. One is perhaps the third and final man born with the power and spirit of Elijah. The last reference said, "Elijah was a man just like us. He prayed earnestly that it would not rain, and it did not rain on the land for three and a half years. Again he prayed, and the heavens gave rain, and the earth produced its crops."

The words faded. My batteries had died.

I bundled up and slept until I was awakened by a sound, deep and penetrating. Wildly I looked around. I was in no position to defend myself from coyotes or bears.

Bears hibernate.

I grinned. *Oh yeah. Well, coyotes. It may be coyotes.*

Or small animals that could creep under the slab and gnaw on you while you helplessly scream in agony.

You! Shut up!

The sky went red. I spotted the source of the deep sound. A great horned was perched in a tree way behind me, a rectangular box with wide-set tufts sticking up. *You'll be laying your eggs in a couple months, huh? Looking for a nest in the cliff?* We watched each other. She was evaluating me lying in the red twilight, ripe and ready as a caught rabbit. *Hey, you're the exact shape and proportion of Leap Castle.* I held up my knife, turning the blade slowly in the light as a threat. *Come after me, friend, and you'll be my breakfast.* The light went, the cold returned, I fell into shadow. The trees turned black and featureless against fading light, then reappeared again once night came, gray and still with yawning hollows behind them, horrible in their blackness. I was anxious that an animal face might appear. I wanted nothing to appear, but I hated the hollow empty loneliness too. *Enough nights alone like this, and a person could go stark raving mad.* I could almost see the shape of Tabonga among the trees, those fake arms and the long, droopy eyes. "Tabonga will die,"

I joked dryly. I thought about Reece climbing Great Oak with me only a couple days ago. I lay down my head tiredly and touched my left thumb and little finger together. *It's a sign of hypothermia if you can't do it, so I'm still okay.* I made my fingers touch and got a huge kick out of it. *Touch, touch, touch.* I tried wiggling my toes and couldn't tell if they were moving. All night I prayed like Elijah for rain.

It was the third day. I had maybe one more day until hunger pangs would start to fade. Until then my guts would be screaming. I couldn't sleep because of the other voice, the one louder than hunger, worse than dead silence, the one whose jeer, *You'll never find it,* still echoed through my head. It was a shock how four little words had messed up my mind so bad.

I was the only person out here, but I definitely wasn't alone.

The thirst was terrible, and I wondered about the world record for surviving without water. Was it two weeks? a month? Could I beat it?

I hadn't used the belt tourniquet—hadn't made that decision yet—but it was lying beside me, ready.

Last night Leap Castle had come again and perched on her tree, her horn-shaped ears listening to the silence, her eyeless face staring down at me. Like she was saying, "I'm Leap Castle. I have the sword and you'll never find it."

Was I going insane?

What are you doing here, Elijah?

I raised my head. *Hey, you sent an angel to bake bread and bring water for the first Elijah when he was out in the wilderness. I read about it in the book of Kings before my batteries died.*

Silence.

Okay, well, to answer your question—nothing. What am I supposed to be doing?

I got a crick in my neck looking up for an answer. After a while I put my head down and tried to sleep, hoping that when I woke, there'd be food by my head like in the book of Kings. But I couldn't sleep. I kept peeking around. *You could send the raven like you did that other time in the Bible. Bread and meat would be good; I'm not particular.* I even wondered if the squirrel I'd seen scampering across the stream would bring the food. I wanted to see how God would do it.

After a while I got to thinking, *Maybe it's like Christmas Eve; if you don't go to sleep, Santa won't come. The presents won't arrive.* I was thinking crazy. I turned my head to the cliff wall and forced myself to sleep, in spite of the maddening sound of water trickling from the rim of the gorge. *Drip, drip, drip.*

Hours later I woke and stretched weakly. There was no food from God. *Hey, you fed the first Elijah. And by the way, Jesus didn't have it this bad when he was in the wilderness. He could move around. He could've gone back to town if he'd wanted.*

I thought long and hard about Jesus out in the wilderness with nothing. No food, no gear, no friends. No nothing. *Can't imagine why you'd do that. Forty days? That's crazy. The sheer willpower it took not to run home. And why? That's my question. Why? There's nothing out here.*

After a long while, I realized that the whole lot of nothing was God's very point. I wouldn't be out here if I wasn't stuck—no news flash there. *If it's you that trapped me here, just tell me what I'm supposed to do, and I'll do it. Then cut me loose.*

High branches waved, but nothing else moved in my narrow little world. I got it at last. *Uh-huh. Got it. Nothing but you and me.*

And me, came the shadow voice, the voiceless voice.

I drifted in and out, tongue parched, mind clear, belly burning. I tracked the movement of the sun across the sky, dreading another night alone.

The raven sailed past.

I'm saved!! He'll bring meat and bread, like he did to the first Elijah. Thank you! Thank you! But the raven glided on as if he hadn't seen me.

"Come back!" I called. "Raven! Come back!" I screamed and yelled and did raven caws until my parched throat quit on me. I slapped the ground furiously. *Come back!*

Talk to me! I wanted to read the Quella bad and wondered if I could squeeze out a little more juice by switching the two batteries around. *Maybe the contacts are dirty. Maybe he wants me to figure out where the sword is, and I'm stuck here until I figure it out.* I switched the batteries around. *Come on, more juice. More juice.* Search options appeared on the little screen. *Yes! Yes!* I rose up on my elbows. *Okay, I'm starting with the four directions. Could you at least tell me which direction, so I can save battery time?*

No answer.

I looked up *north* and gave up after a few tries. There was nothing to the north of me anyway but farmland. Dowland wouldn't hide anything on another guy's farm—too risky. *Okay, I'm looking up* south, *and you know I may be running out of juice.*

The first fifteen references were no help. The sixteenth was Deuteronomy 33:23: "Naphtali is abounding with the favor of the LORD and is full of his blessing; he will inherit southward to the lake." The footnote said that *Naphtali* was derived from the word *struggle* or *fight.* The one who fights, struggles—that would be me—will inherit something. I remembered what he'd told me before: that he'd give me a secret treasure. Did this confirm it? Camp Mudj's lake was due south of Gilead. *The sword's in Silver Lake?! Southward to the lake and close to where Old Pilgrim Church once stood, where Stan Dowland had first buried the armor! It's been lying there while paddleboats floated over it all summer—right under my nose the whole time? Is the helmet there too?*

The Quella died again. I switched the batteries once more, but it seemed shut down for good.

Southward to the lake! I know where the rest of it is! I cocooned in my sleeping bag and celebrated my moment of glory. I'd found it. So Dowland had given up on his little piece-by-piece riddle and decided to dump the pieces at random? Had he intended to put a clue to finding the helmet with the shoes of peace before Francine stole them from his house? Was there a clue to another mystery at the bottom of the lake? I didn't care. Magdeline could have all the mysteries and scandals she wanted. I had the armor of God!

In the middle of figuring out what had been going on in Dowland's demented mind, it occurred to me with a dull gnawing in my stomach that if I didn't make it out of Gilead, the others would never find the armor.

I don't want the secret to die with me, God. Don't let me die—for the sake of the armor. You can't let me die.

He doesn't need you.

I'm not talking to you! I said with contempt to the shadow voice. *I can leave a message scratched in the dirt or I can lie here and die.* I considered my options. *Hey, God, if you don't let me live, the secret will die with me. So forget about that message in the dirt I just mentioned. I changed my mind!* I was bargaining, knowing deep inside that the evil one was right. *God doesn't need me. He never did. I'm as helpless and useless as a roach under the heel of a shoe.* I looked heavenward and called hoarsely, "Is this your plan for me? Is it?! Tell me!!"

Exhausted, I fell asleep for an hour or so and woke with no feeling at all in my foot. I pushed and kept pushing until I felt pressure and a little burning. The pressure had been there the whole time, but I hadn't thought about it. *I can feel my heel. It's still alive.* Encouraged—even though a feeling foot was a bad thing if you're going to have to amputate it—I pressed my heel into the rock and enjoyed the pain. *My heel.* Suddenly I was back at the Cliffs of Morte that moment I'd run to grab Reece at the edge. I relived how my foot had tipped back over a six-hundred-foot drop into the North Atlantic, how my heel had felt rock where there was none. *He didn't want me to die then. Maybe he doesn't now. You want me to live? You do, don't you?* I laughed out loud, a raw, hoarse bark.

You sound like Dowland.

I'm not him! I answered the shadowy whisper. *I never will be him! I won't make his mistakes,* I insisted, though I'd never exactly figured what Dowland's mistake was.

If Francine was right, he'd never really been interested in the real armor of God—truth and peace and faith and stuff like that. Yeah, he'd preached sermons on it, but it had never sunk in. Dowland had gone loony trying to find a treasure he had within reach all along.

Insanity runs in the family, boy. Self-destruction is in your genes.

I'm not listening to you.

A treasure almost within reach—but not quite. Like your food and water. It's right there; you can see it.

I looked at my backpack. So near. Rage and regret boiled up in me.

Can't reach it, though, can you?

God, make him stop!!

For hours I mulled over what could have gone wrong with Dowland and with the whole town in general, why all the churches died out except for a sad little storefront congregation with the drab Christmas decorations and the long name. Magdeline, Ohio, had possessed the armor of God for decades and had never used it. It was an average go-nowhere-do-nothing kind of town, and that's what it would always be. Dowland never learned what Reece knew from the very first: that the armor itself wasn't the point. The power of our treasure was in the message, not the metal. A free treasure, anybody could claim it and be saved!

I don't want this secret to die with me. I rubbed my hands together, thawing my fingers. With the knife I scratched in the dirt: SOTERION LAKE deut33. The clan would understand. *Soterion,* Greek for *salvation.* They'd find the verse and figure out that the helmet of salvation or the sword of the Lord was in the lake. They'd understand. Relief and joy flooded through me. They'd find it. They'd complete the quest.

Lying there, stinking and freezing, my body screamed for water. I cursed at the raven for leaving me. Dreading what God had lined up for me later, I suddenly had a revelation as blinding as lightning: *it's more important that Marcus, Rob, Reece, and Mei find the armor than whether or not I live. Its purpose has to be fulfilled—arming a generation for the Day of Evil. That's the most important thing of all.*

I was shocked that the armor meant more to me than my life. *More than my very own life!*

Chapter 9

DO *you want me to lay here and die, God? Or do you want me to saw off my foot and crawl home and never run again? Which one is it? Is someone coming? Are they searching Telanoo right now? Or are they questioning the Stallards? Is news spreading across the Midwest that a boy from Magdeline is missing and thought to be headed for Chicago? If I wait too late to amputate, I won't have the strength to go through with it. But what if I do it and five minutes later they find me? I don't know what to do!*

Exactly.

I could almost see the evil one grinning at my predicament. He sounded a lot like Justin Brill.

I seethed. *Don't you get it? I'm not listening to you!*

But I *was* listening. And as I played the conversations over and over and over, the difference in God's words and his got more and more distinct. The difference was in the content and in the tone. I felt pure hate coming from the shadowy messages. But I'd always sensed God's love for me in his words—even the time in October when God said he'd let me see my enemy and his voice was stern and a little scary.

I knew it in the same way that I knew how Reece felt about me, even when she was rolling her eyes over something about the Bible that I was too dense to get.

I recognized the disgust in the evil one's tone because

of how Justin Brill was always making fun of me. *Wow. I would never have seen the difference so clearly if I'd never heard Brill's slams and name-calling: "Hey, Nature Boy, eat any roadkill lately? Hey, Creek, you and Elliston . . . mumble mumble . . . heh, heh, heh."* How he leered and jeered at Reece and me. I had something he didn't. He was jealous! And so was the evil one. He was jealous because I had God.

God had been using something bad to teach me an important rule: good could come from bad.

"See how it works out, Elijah?" Reece's cheery voice echoed in my head from our golden time at the top of Great Oak. *"If you hadn't ignored me, I wouldn't have gotten mad, and I wouldn't be here. He always works it out."*

I rested my forehead on my hand and smiled in amazement. *El-Telan-Yah, do you mean that you let Justin Brill give me grief so I'd recognize the voice of the evil one when it spoke? Was that the plan all along? Well, that's pretty weird—but cool. Funny, I never thought I'd be grateful to Brill for anything. That's wild how you can make bad stuff work out for good. Like Mei being sent back to Japan so she could be with us in Ireland. But now that I know, God . . . now that I get it, can you make the evil one go away? And if I die out here, please don't let Brill end up with Reece. That would be sick and wrong.*

It was mid-afternoon and my spirits rose again. I scratched a map of the world in the dirt around "SOTERION LAKE deut33" without even knowing why. Seven continents, seven seas. I quit drawing when the shivering and fumbling of my hand got worse—a sign of hypothermia.

I fluffed the sleeping bag and tried to rise up and stretch more. I edged into the sunlight as much as possible while it lasted. For someone like me who couldn't ride in a car for a few hours without going berserk, this was my worst nightmare. Stuck—like a butterfly in a bug collection. I rubbed my arms and my legs as far down as I could to keep circulation going.

The burning throb in my foot was beyond measuring. Every move was more awkward and, as I got colder, every effort more exhausting. I fought sleep for fear I wouldn't wake up. When I couldn't fight it anymore, I gave in and thought of Reece, how she turned the bad to good, her crutches into wings. . . .

She stood on the rim of Gilead, which was also the edge of the Cliffs of Morte. The wind whipped her hair wildly around her face. The others were there: Rob and Marcus and Mei and Sahara too. We stood safely back from the edge. Reece was an eagle and an angel. She had a message for us. As we waited to hear it, she lifted her wings. The wind caught them, and off she went over the edge. Mei screamed. My heart stopped. We ran to the edge, threw ourselves on our bellies, and looked down in horror.

Below us she glided like one of the gulls—swooping, banking off away from the cliff, circling back. When I saw that she was going to be okay, I dropped my head to the ground and cried with relief.

I woke sniffling. It was the dead of night. Drained from my feelings about the dream, it was a minute before I realized that there was tapping all around me. *Taptaptaptaptaptap.* I looked around at the dull charcoal sky. There was Leap Castle, perched in a tree much closer than before. *She's moving in.* The tapping was rain . . . no . . . it was sleet.

An ice storm? God, what are you thinking? Sure it's water, but frozen water. I can't get to it!

At the first gray light of dawn, I raised my head and looked around. Every branch, every dead blade of weed and prairie grass was glazed over. Frozen stiff.

He's teasing you.

I ignored the voice, switched the batteries in the Quella again, and checked the screen in the pearly light of dawn. But it was no good.

Reece's poem! I hadn't brought it out because I would have wanted to burn it for the heat. I knew I'd see the paper, handle it, and imagine the warmth. I wouldn't be able to resist. If I needed to use the knife on myself soon, I would want to sterilize the blade with fire. *Read now; burn later. I have to hear a human voice.* I dug the paper from my pocket and held it to the southeastern sky. I imagined that she was reading it to me.

"A poem from English class," she said. *"I thought of you when I read it. So here it is. 'The Light of Stars' from* Voices of the Night *by Henry Wadsworth Longfellow."* She cleared her throat and read:

The night is come, but not too soon;
And sinking silently,
All silently, the little moon
Drops down behind the sky.

There is no light in earth or heaven
But the cold light of stars;
And the first watch of night is given
To the red planet Mars.

Is it the tender star of love?
The star of love and dreams?
O no! from that blue tent above,
A hero's armor gleams.

And earnest thoughts within me rise,
When I behold afar,
Suspended in the evening skies,
The shield of that red star.

O star of strength! I see thee stand
And smile upon my pain;
Thou beckonest with thy mailed hand,
And I am strong again.

Within my breast there is no light
But the cold light of stars;

I give the first watch of the night
To the red planet Mars.

The star of the unconquered will,
He rises in my breast,
Serene, and resolute, and still,
And calm, and self-possessed.

I stopped a minute to rest my arms. Leaning the side of my face to the cold ground, I looked up at the pale sky for a morning star. A few night stars still shone. I watched them twinkle, wondering if any of them was the planet Mars. I let Reece's voice read the rest of the poem:

And thou, too, whosoe'er thou art,
That readest this brief psalm,
As one by one thy hopes depart,
Be resolute and calm.

O fear not in a world like this,
And thou shalt know erelong,
Know how sublime a thing it is
To suffer and be strong.

Dazed with emotions I couldn't even name, I pulled my cocoon around me and stared at my frozen world. Slowly the sky brightened. Light grew on Gilead's ice-covered trees, their limbs bowing under the weight. Then the sun came out and cast golden beams down the gorge. Little by little the ice came alive—sparkling, blinding, and beautiful. Every twig and leaf and stone was a glittering rainbow. *I'm in Heaven.* I couldn't speak or even think a word. No words like *golden* or *crystal* could describe it because it wasn't just beautiful. There was life in it, in every frozen drop of water, every limb, groaning and crackling under weight of ice. The sun rose brighter. Every branch, every blade of grass, every bush became a trillion diamonds of blue, turquoise, gold, orange—a zillion rainbows.

I lay there in awe, drinking in the light show.

And the trees started to drip. I got up on my elbows to watch and listen. He was answering my prayer—not just from a cloud a few thousand feet up—from the sun's fire ninety-three million miles away. He was sweating the trees, turning sleet into rain from across the solar system! The verse came to me from the first Elijah's story: The god who answers by fire—he is God.

I got it! I got the message of the ice storm, El-Telan-Yah. I'm frozen too; the slab is weighing me down, but there's still life in me. I got the message, but . . . where's my water? I can't reach it.

Wait, came the answer.

He's teasing you, Elijah. . . .

Trees cried and crackled as the morning went on, dripping, dripping. Diamonds falling like rain—diamonds of every color. The sun went behind a cloud, a big puffy white one with a blue-black underside. The dripping and crackling slowed for the next several minutes. Then the melting stopped. The zillion rainbows went away. *He's in control. He makes it start and stop. He can do anything he wants. That's what he's saying.*

The cloud drifted away and my world lit up again. The trees started cracking once more. As the ice melted and fell to the ground, their limbs began to rise. It reminded me of church, when the congregation bows together for prayer and then raises their heads together. I watched for hours as trees ever so slowly lifted their heads and arms to the sky. I missed church—the row of kids, the chocolate milk and donuts at Bible study, the songs, the stained glass windows, the minister's jokes and stories and lessons.

I understood now why sun worshipers built tombs like Newgrange. Every inch of the natural world depended on the sun and responded to its fire. I looked at the picture of the world I'd drawn in the dirt and thought about Mei and Sahara and all the millions of people in the world who worship nature. *If you don't know him, sure, why not worship the sun?*

Where's my water, God?

Rubbing my legs to keep them alive, I read the poem over until I had it almost by heart. I couldn't believe how clear I was thinking, how sharp my memory was. I tucked the page into my shirt, slept, and felt warmth again. It was mid-afternoon. The feeling of comfort returned.

Splat.

A drop of water hit the ground two feet from my head.

Splat. Splat.

I reached out my hand. *Blup. Blup.* Water dripped into my palm! I looked up. The sun had reached an icicle suspended from a crack in the ledge. *Water!* Painstakingly I gathered drips of water in my hand. *Patience, patience . . .* I lapped out of my filthy palm and reached greedily for more. The icicle was about two feet long and a couple inches thick at the top. Three glasses of water were up there waiting to drip into my hand!

That won't keep you alive.

Before I could prepare my mind for another night of darkness, the sun moved behind the rim of the gorge. It was December 22, the shortest day of the year. By 6:00 it would be nightfall. The same sun, which had lit up the passage tomb of Newgrange on the other side of the planet, had given me another day of life and clean drinking water. *Thank you, God.*

The light left. The dripping stopped. The sky turned orange, the shadows purple.

Sun doesn't always mean life. In deserts the sun means death. Today in Gilead, though, I had water from fire. Ice needs fire. Everything needs everything else to work. Fire is life. It purifies, cooks, destroys, warms, and sterilizes. Earth, wind, fire, and water—that's all there is. *That's all I am: earth and water.*

And soul.

Yeah. I know I'm more than this aching, stinking body. I'm eternal. Even if I die.

Now I'm not ragging on Dom's Eight Lessons or anything, but the lessons I was learning from God while trapped under that slab had to number in the hundreds. Or thousands. My mind was razor sharp; my body was screaming for release. My foot was probably dead.

I got a little more water from the rock above me. Reece read the poem to me again and again inside my head. I reviewed my life. I tried to remember as much of the Bible as I could, wishing I knew more. I thirsted to hear his voice. A thousand times I said to God, *Get me out of this and I'm yours.*

I wondered what Mom and Dad were doing about me. *They've questioned Reece by now. She'll think I hid out in Council Cliffs like the two Delaware Indian boys. When she went down at Hermits' Cave, we'd talked about how I could live out there. They're probably scouring Council Cliffs. How long will that take?*

I woke up terrified, thinking I'd gone blind. I didn't remember going to sleep. It was dark. Leap Castle was back, closer than ever, her black, square body and pointy horn-ears haunting me. She was one measly owl, but her presence and her shape terrified me beyond words. She didn't move. It wasn't natural. *It's an owl, for crying out loud. Get a grip.* But I couldn't. Inside I screamed, *I can't take any more! I'm going crazy! At first light, if I'm alive, I will get that knife and do what must be done! If you don't want me to, you better stop me!*

"Elijaaaah!"

My mind surfaced in a flash. *Had someone called my name?* I listened through a blowing snow squall. It was day five.

"Elijaaaaah!"

Rob! It's Rob!! I'm rescued! I'm saved!!

My heart leaped. I raised my head, arched my back, opened my mouth, and cried out. But only a short, low-pitched bark came out. I tried again. And again. I'd shot my dried-out vocal cords screaming a couple nights before. My voice was gone. Rob's calls got louder. I heard him talking to someone and guessed that Marcus was with him. Frantically I looked around for something to make noise with. I had nothing but the knife and a rock. Aching and cold, I got up stiffly on my one free knee and reached for the rock. When their voices got closer, I'd throw it into the stream and get their attention. It was one of my only three weapons—rock, belt, knife—but I had to be heard.

"Elijah!" Rob's call was close.

They're above me! The sun came out, and two long narrow shadows fell across Gilead. I barked, but they couldn't hear. *You can see me if you circle around to the other side! You can see my gear if you lean way over. Circle around, Marcus. Circle like we did at Hermits' Cave. I'm right below you!* I screamed inside. *You'll see me from the other side. Marcus! Rob! Drop down on your bellies like we did at the Cliffs of Morte. I'm right under you!!*

I lifted the rock and hurled it toward the creek. My pitch was weak and shaky. The rock fell short and landed in a soft bush. *Bmff!* For a moment I heard nothing. They were listening. Had they heard the rock? They mumbled to each other. The sun peeked out, their shadows appeared, and then they moved away. *No!!!* Once more I tried to yell. Hardly a wheeze came out, not enough sound against the wind. *Don't leave!* I threw myself forward and slapped the ground over and over. *Slap, slap, slap! Listen to me!*

Marcus's voice called, "Hey, Creeeeek!" Then it faded out, "Where are you, Cree . . . ?" In the distance other voices were calling my name. Dad had organized a manhunt, but they'd missed me. A few stray flakes landed on the back of my outstretched hand. I licked them off and dropped my head to the cold ground.

Fire. If only I'd had fire. Smoke. Flame. Smell.

The day passed. I stayed sane thinking of Reece's poem and what Bible verses I could remember. *No one else is coming. They've probably decided I was in Chicago. I'll die in the shirt that I was baptized in. That's why I wore it. That's why.*

All voices went silent for a long while, even my own.

Then . . . *Hey, what about the third Elijah? In the Quella's footnotes, didn't it say that some believed that a third Elijah would come at the end?* As the light faded again, I switched the batteries once more, cleaning the contact points with a corner of my shirt. This time I got juice.

"'And I will give power to my two witnesses, and they will

prophesy for 1,260 days, clothed in sackcloth.' These are the two olive trees and the two lampstands that stand before the Lord of the earth. If anyone tries to harm them, fire comes from their mouths and devours their enemies. This is how anyone who wants to harm them must die. These men have power to shut up the sky so that it will not rain during the time they are prophesying; and they have power to turn the waters into blood and to strike the earth with every kind of plague as often as they want. Now when they have finished their testimony, the beast that comes up from the Abyss will attack them, and overpower and kill them. Their bodies will lie in the street of the great city, which is figuratively called Sodom and Egypt, where also their Lord was crucified. For three and a half days men from every people, tribe, language and nation will gaze on their bodies and refuse them burial. The inhabitants of the earth will gloat over them and will celebrate by sending each other gifts, because these two prophets had tormented those who live on the earth. But after the three and a half days a breath of life from God entered them, and they stood on their feet, and terror struck those who saw them."

If I'm the third Elijah, I explained to God, *then I have to die in the streets of Jerusalem. I can't die here. And it has to be after a whole bunch of days of preaching on the streets like that preacher in Dublin. A thousand days.*

It gave me a weird kind of hope. I closed the Quella and stared across the stream, imagining what I'd say if I ever got to preach in Jerusalem. At mid-afternoon the comfort came the same as it had on the other days.

If you want me to cut off my foot and crawl out of here, I will. But you know what that means. I'll never run track. And I won't be much good to Dad at the camp. I don't get it. Do you want me to be like Reece so I'll have faith like hers? Is that your plan? Whatever you want me to do, I will do it! Just TELL ME!!! Just don't leave me here wondering.

He's not listening.

"Yes, he is! He is!" I said it over and over, slapping the ground until I was exhausted and my parched throat burned.

I lay there picturing where I was, as if from above, as if I were a raven. I drew a map of Telanoo in the dirt: Owl Woods, the streams, Devil's Cranium. I raised up. *Hey . . . if Devil's Cranium due east of me was the actual skull of Satan crammed face-first into the cliff side of Telanoo—which it isn't, that's crazy, but if it was—then he's looking through the earth right at me.*

A wild chill of horror shot through me.

Stop it, Creek! You're losing it. Keep your mind on what's real. This is not a cheap horror movie. Focus on what's real.

"Hey, Wingate," I said, "what's the weather like where you are? Hey, Mom, what's for dinner? Hey, Skidmore," I wheezed as I drifted off in the cold darkness for the last time, "you always thought I was a pyro? Wait till I come hobbling out of these woods! Fire will be my middle name."

Chapter 10

I woke to the sound of music. I thought it was a hiker. My brain asked, *Where's that coming from? A hunter with a radio? A hunter singing? Crazy. You're imagining it. But it's not a radio. Where is that coming from? It's . . .* It was coming from inside my chest. A quiet voice was singing that song from Ireland about the days of Elijah. *What in the world?* my brain asked and then answered itself. *It's my spirit.*

I lay there in my dirty cocoon, my body cold, my mind paper-thin but razor sharp while my spirit sang as happy as a kid at a picnic. I listened, amazed. *How awesome it that? That's my soul singing while I'm dying.* I cautioned my brain to hush. *Don't think too much. You'll stifle it. Shut up and listen.*

The little voice got quiet and reverent. Then another voice spoke. *Put it on.*

What?

Put it on.

He meant the armor. How?

Pray.

The singer got quiet and waited.

Okay, God . . . My mind started in: *belt of truth. The* omen. *Your word is truth, and it says that you are with me always.* The truth for me was—I could see so clearly now—that even if I died here, I wouldn't die alone. He would never leave. I had my spirit to sing to me in the final moments if that should happen. Still I was terrified. I went on.

Breastplate of righteousness. You guard my heart with your goodness. I don't have to be good enough. I never did. Nobody does. You're the Lamb over me. The gi.

I remembered that it was Christmas Eve day, when God's Lamb was born to die.

Next are the shoes of peace. Langundowagan. *O God, this is hard. How does a person have peace when he's slowly starving to death?*

Be still, and know that I am God.

Well . . . okay. I've sort of been doing that. The next is the shield of faith. I do believe. I do have creidim.

I felt a little fake. Most of the things I was praying were things I'd heard Reece or Marcus or the Dublin preacher talk about—nothing I'd thought up myself. *But I still believe it,* I insisted. *I'm not just saying this stuff. Okay. Helmet of salvation.* Soterion. *It's southward to the lake and with the sword, I hope, and the arm piece. Lord, I wore that helmet once—all night at The Cedars—remember?*

I realized at that moment the only reason Dowland hadn't taken me out in Telanoo was that I'd kept the helmet on all night. I saw his intentions now, clear as day. He hated that he'd never found the sword and that the armor hadn't worked like he wanted. He hated that I might figure out what he'd missed—like a spoiled kid who says, "I don't want it, but I don't want you to have it either." Maybe he'd thrown it into the lake because he knew that I was the third Elijah. Yes, he'd written my name three times in his journals and crossed out two. Whether Dowland had kept his hands off me because he thought the helmet was magical or cursed didn't matter. Truth was that the helmet of salvation saved my life—not in just a spiritual sense, but in a physical sense. God had protected my life through Dowland's superstitions. He'd saved me in every way, even before I knew him. *I'm saved whether I'm alive or dead. I'll go to Heaven.*

In a real way, I'd already been rescued. The peace that I'd lacked a moment ago flooded through me. *I'm okay. I'm okay no matter what. The whole armor works together. One piece helps the other. Hey, God, if I die, tell Reece where the helmet and sword are, okay? Tell her personally. She'd like that, and she deserves to know even more than me. Promise me that you'll let her see it.*

I started thinking about her again, how we'd kissed at the top of Great Oak . . .

Sword, he reminded me firmly. *Put it on.*

Oh yeah. The sword of the Lord. Well, I'd hoped to see it . . . just once.

I sighed at the silence, hoping that he'd throw me a hint. *Okay, here goes. I'll take the sword in hand even though I've never seen it. The sword is your Word; your Word is truth. Your words have power. By the way, I'd be reading it right now, but the batteries are dead. A little ironic, isn't it?*

I lay there thinking of Scriptures. *"Even though I walk through the valley of the shadow of death, I will fear no evil, for you are with me." "In the beginning God created the heavens and the earth." "God is light; in him there is no darkness at all."*

How I wished that I were on my back! Like when I was a kid and would lie in the grass and watch the clouds floating past. *I'm so helpless this way, so defenseless.* I longed for a patch of sunlight to warm my sleeping bag. *Sun, where are you?* I looked up hoping the clouds would clear. Something caught my eye. I thought at first that it was a broken branch. Then I thought it was a piece of rope draped in the top of a tree near the cliff wall. *That's no rope . . . oh no . . .* Slithering along a branch with her midsection sagging between two limbs was Bloocifer.

You! I sneered.

I wished for my rock, the one I'd hurled into the bush to signal the guys. All I had left was the belt and knife. *If I throw and miss, I'll have nothing. I have to keep both for the amputation!* Frantically I dug at the ground for clods to throw. The dirt crumbled in my hands.

She saw me and stopped. We locked eyes—her cold, sideways, Liam-looking glare fixed on me as she moved down the tree. I could just tell that she hated me for caging her and stealing her babies. She wasn't afraid of me; she was sizing up my situation and thinking revenge. Did she know that I was trapped?

I was afraid, but it was a different kind of fear. It was around me but not in me.

"You're just a snake," I whispered, "a belly-crawling

reptile. You're nothing to me. You're not poisonous. Sure, you could bite, and it would hurt like heck, but you couldn't kill me." *Blue racers are constrictors,* I reminded myself, *but they don't strangle. They kill prey by pressing down on them, swallowing them whole.*

Like the slab that's pressing down on you, killing you ever so slowly, she seemed to say.

I held up my knife. *You bite me; I'll cut you. We both lose. So go away.*

Unless . . . unless she waited a few days until I was too weak. Then she'd win. *Does she know? Does she smell my weakness?*

She slid to the ground, raised up like a cobra, and froze. Her tail rattled, a soft whirring sound.

Ten yards. She'd be on me in two or three seconds. "You're just a snake," I said grittily. "I caught you, and you'd still be in that cage if those jerk college kids hadn't been goofing off." Using my anger for strength, I went on, "I took your babies, sold them, and then I used the money to search for the sword of the Lord."

Didn't find it, did you?

You're hallucinating, Creek, I told myself.

Keep your wits, came a strong, steady voice.

I will, I answered.

You'll never find it, came Liam's voice from that bookstore in Dublin. *You're starving.*

"'Man does not live on bread alone,'" I answered out

loud, "'but on every word that comes from the mouth of God.' That's the sword of the Lord. The Word. It doesn't matter what you do to me, Bloo. That sword will cut you and your kind to ribbons in the end."

Who was I talking to: a snake, a demon, Satan himself, or just my own raw imagination? It didn't matter. I was weak . . . but somehow strong.

I kept my eye on Bloocifer until my neck cramped so bad that I had to rest it. I showed her my knife blade, turning it in the light. *Though I walk through the valley of the shadow of death, I will fear no evil, for you are with me.*

When I looked up, she was gone. *Uh-oh. How am I supposed to sleep tonight? Tomorrow night? Or the next, if there is a next? She'll slither into my sleeping bag. I have no defenses!!!*

You have the armor.

It's not real! I threw my head onto my folded arms. *I need something real! A rock or my bow and arrow! I need something REAL!*

The silence was deafening. For an hour I waited for a word. Had I offended him and his armor? Had he left me? No, I could still feel him there, waiting patiently for me to figure out things by myself.

I'm sorry.

Your struggle will not be against flesh and blood, Elijah, but against the rulers, against the authorities, against the powers of this dark world and against the spiritual forces of evil in the heavenly realms.

My mind was still on Bloocifer. *Snakes hibernate in bunches, sometimes in the sides of cliffs,* I informed God, *thirty, fifty, even a hundred at a time.* With growing horror my eyes went up the side of the cliff. *They're above me, aren't they? They've been there the whole time, a whole nest of 'em, just waiting to come out to sun themselves on the warm rocks.*

They're all around, he answered matter-of-factly. He wasn't just talking about snakes. He meant the spiritual forces. I was learning by now that when God speaks, he often speaks in layers or riddles. His words are three-dimensional. They can mean two or three things at once. His words move.

They are not your first concern.

The snakes or the forces of evil? I asked. He meant both. *I figured as much. I'm starting to see, El-Telan-Yah.*

What are you doing here, Elijah? he asked me a second time.

I'm starting to see.

The story of Adam and Eve made perfect sense now. I was sorry that I'd doubted it and even sorrier that I'd ever asked to see the dark side. I heard Dom's voice warning me: "Better watch what you ask God for. You just might get it."

I fought off agonizing weariness—afraid that I'd slip into unconsciousness and not wake up. I'd had nightmares: I was Salem, shot with arrows . . . I was Stan Dowland, filled with rage and regret, watching someone else wear the armor of God . . . Reece and Brill were together . . . my dad was giving up on me . . . rocks were falling on me. I dreaded the dreams, but I couldn't keep my eyes open. When darkness fell for the sixth time, it didn't matter anyway. I was in a pitch-black Hell of bone-aching cold and thirst. Numbness was creeping up my leg. Animals could be chewing it off, and I'd never know. I hadn't felt sensation in my foot since . . . I didn't know when.

Okay. This is it! If at first light I'm alive, I will take my knife in hand and do what must be done. I mean it this time. While I have the strength to do it. I pray that I have the strength to crawl out of Gilead, across Telanoo, and through Owl Woods to home. Home. I'll hug Mom and Dad, hug the twins, hobble through town, find Marcus and Rob, find Reece and kiss her again. Then we'll all meet at Florence's for grits and bacon. Yeah.

Chapter 11

WHIIIRRRRR.

My head shot up, wobbling; my mind panicked. *Whirring? What is it?* My eyes strained to see into the blackness. Night clouds lay low and heavy; there was no light at all. *Was it the wings of Leap Castle zooming in to gouge out my eyes?* I ducked. *Was it Bloocifer's rattling tail, warning me of a strike?* I grabbed my belt and whipped it out blindly in all directions. The whirring was loud and steady. Horror gripped my mind. Lights flashed before my eyes. Terror surrounded me. *No . . . no, not that! It's all hundred of them!? Vicious blue racers circling me in the blackness, signaling attack! God, are you there?! ARE YOU THERE? DON'T LEAVE ME!!*

The sound got louder with a *thoo-thoo-thoo* thumping rhythmically underneath the whirring—like eagles' wings pumping the air in flight.

It's . . . a helicopter! A copter!

Fumbling and frantic, I whipped out Reece's poem and wadded it up. I ripped off my damp shirt. I got the matches from my pocket and struck one, setting the pile on fire. My hands scrambled in the darkness and found bits of straw and a few leaves to add to my pathetic little blaze. I circled it with my arms to protect it from the wind. *Come on, copter. Look down; I'm here!!* My hopes soared. *I'm saved!!*

The helicopter roared over the narrow rim of Gilead and headed west. The little fire sputtered. *Wait! I'm here!* In a few minutes the copter doubled back and hovered a few seconds, but my fire had died down to a quivering pile of red ashes. My world went black for the last time; the helicopter moved on. My head dropped to the cold ground. Blindly, I waved my hand over the warm embers, feeling their brief comfort. *What more?* I asked desperately. *What more?*

I heard movement in the dry grass across the stream. *Footsteps? Slow and cautious. Not human,* I judged with a kind of strange, distant objectivity. *It's a medium-sized animal, four-legged. A coyote. They found me. And there'll be more.*

I got the belt, worked it around my left leg just below the knee—that was as far down as I could reach—and yanked. *Awkward angle. Not tight enough. I'll rest a little and try again. Tighter. Cut off the blood that hasn't crystallized.*

"I'll need your help to do this," I spoke into the night. "Don't they call you the great physician? Well, give me what you got: anesthetic, a steady hand, whatever. That helicopter sweep was my last hope. But I'm not staying here with a nest of racers over my head, coyotes circling, and my family thinking I'm dead, while the helmet of salvation and sword of the Lord rust at the bottom of the lake. I have to do something. I've waited on you long enough."

To spite my impossible circumstances, I scraped the ground where I'd written "SOTERION LAKE deut33" and drawn the map. *If there's a message about the armor of God, I'm delivering it in person.* I didn't care that I was dirtying and dulling the blade. *I've got no fire to sterilize it, got no feeling anyway, so what does it matter?* I rested awhile and then drew the belt another notch tighter. The faintest hint of dawn teased the horizon. A bright star burned above me. I wondered if it was Mars and quoted Reece's poem: *As one by one thy hopes depart, be resolute and calm.* I bundled myself for my last hours as a two-legged boy and slept, so I'd be strong at first light.

I felt a hand on my shoulder. "Elijah! Dear God! Elijah!" came a booming voice. "He's alive! Give me a hand, quick!"

The voice seemed vaguely familiar. I was awake. Rescued.

"Russ! We got him, man. We got him!"

There was Dom kneeling beside me and my dad running up behind. Beside Dad was Donovan of all people, the tennis-pro type I'd first met at the Stallards' office in Chicago, who'd helped us retrieve the breastplate of righteousness. Behind them came two rescue squad guys I recognized from when Reece had gotten hurt in Hermits' Cave.

Dad's voice was choked when he dropped down and looked me in the face, his expression full of shock and dismay. "We've got you, son. You're okay now. We've got you. Hang on."

"I'm okay," I croaked. "I need water."

A canteen appeared. I tipped my head around and they poured it into my mouth. Never, ever was there a better taste. Never. Beautiful, beautiful water.

Then came a flood of questions and comments. Dom asked, "How'd you get yourself into such a fix, boy?" and proceeded to order the rescue squad around, how they could leverage the rock up little by little, brace it underneath, and pull me out. He joked about how bad I stank. He and Donovan talked like they knew each other; they surveyed the slab and my tools and exchanged words out of earshot. Dad never left my side.

The squad did their thing—taking my vital signs, checking for broken bones, and getting me warm.

With a lot of heaving and yelling, the slab was raised and Dad pulled me out. Everyone marveled that my foot wasn't crushed. But when the shoe and sock came off, we all saw what a nasty shade of blue gray it was. Dad's jaw clamped, and he said, "Let's get him to Columbus. Come on!"

They had to carry me a long way because the helicopter hadn't been able to land in Telanoo—too rough and scraggly. They'd found a pasture on a neighboring farm. Once we were strapped in and the helicopter took off, I asked Dad, "How'd you know where I was?"

He nodded to Dom and Donovan. "They saw your fire."

The doctors weren't sure they could save the foot. Dad cried. I said, "It'll be okay. Don't worry." Nurses referred to me as "the missing boy," so I figured I'd made the papers.

Mom went all to pieces once she got there with the twins. She cried and apologized for being depressed and yelling at me. She blamed herself for my running off. I had to talk her down from that ledge. "No, Mom. It was an accident. I was doing survival stuff, and a rock fell on me. No one's to blame."

The twins hugged me hard and patted my head like I was one of their baby dolls. It was kind of cute. They were glad I wasn't *weebid*. Whatever that meant.

"I'm very un-*weebid*," I said with a weak smile.

Grandma Creek had come up before Christmas when she heard I was missing. She swabbed her eyes and planted a hard kiss on my forehead. "Don't you ever go off without telling someone, my precious boy, no matter how old you get! No man is an island!"

I was hooked up to machines, scrubbed down, whispered over, fed liquids, poked, and prodded. The sheets and pillows and warmed blankets were pure Heaven. I concentrated on the bed linens to take my mind off the searing pain in my foot as feeling returned.

Then I heard other voices as if from far away. Rob, Marcus, and Reece were out in the hall. Mom was out there telling them that they couldn't stay long, that I might be sleeping and needed my rest.

"Hey!" I croaked. "Let 'em in."

They circled around me with strange, uncertain looks on their faces. They'd probably heard the news that I might lose my foot. Rob peeked under the sheet and nearly retched when he saw it. Reece pulled a chair up close to me and grasped my hand. She pressed her head to my hand and closed her eyes, praying. Then her eyes opened on me, sad and scared and intense. "Tell us everything."

"I was working on a place," I rasped. "Gilead. For the clan. Big rock slid; I got caught under it. Six days."

They helped me get the story out. When they got the whole picture—that I'd been facedown on the cold ground without food and water except for one big icicle, that I'd kept my sanity with the Quella until it died, then with the Bible verses I remembered, and finally with the poem—Reece covered her face and cried.

Rob cried guiltily, "We were right there! During the manhunt we called and called!"

I pointed to my throat. "Dried out. Couldn't talk."

Marcus didn't say much, watching me with a mix of disbelief and admiration.

Reece said, "When we heard you were missing, the three of us got together every afternoon and prayed. We prayed so hard right after school let out. Then when Christmas break started, we called each other at the same time. Church had a prayer chain going and my Devo club did too."

"Thanks." I paused, remembering the feelings of warmth and peace that came about the same time every day. "Every afternoon?"

"Like clockwork."

"Wow . . . I felt that. About 3:00 every day. I *felt* that."

She huffed. "Well, of course you did. It's *prayer!*"

Marcus peeked at my foot under the covers and made a face. "Whoa. Serious damage. That has to hurt."

"Right now it feels like someone stuck my foot in boiling oil." Soberly I thought, *like one foot in Hell.*

Reece said, "We'll go so you can rest."

I grasped her hand. "Don't leave."

Marcus and Rob exchanged looks. I explained, "Talk to me, guys. I need human voices. Talk."

Rob said, "Everyone had a different theory about what happened to you. It was crazy."

"Stallards?" I asked.

"That's what your parents thought. They found an address and thought you'd run off up there. It's been in the news and everything."

"Not good," I said, thinking of Cravens. "Call the Stallards; tell them I'm okay."

"Dad already did," Marcus said.

Reece glanced out the door to see where Mom was and then turned back to me. "Your mom thought for sure that I knew something, that I was keeping a secret. She kept calling all of us to ask if we'd heard from you. They were sure you'd gone to Chicago. But I knew you wouldn't go off without telling . . . *someone.*" She grinned shyly.

Rob said, "The police grilled the Stallards, staged a manhunt through Telanoo, questioned Justin Brill—"

"Brill?" I croaked out a laugh. "You're kidding."

Marcus shrugged. "Which was my theory. But Reece

kept telling Officer Taylor that you were back there in the woods. When the manhunt turned up zip, it was her idea to fly over at night. She was relentless about it."

She leaned in even more intently. "If you were back there and alive, there'd be a fire, I just knew it. So I made the police fly over at night."

I laughed. "You *made* the police fly over?"

"I did," she beamed.

"True," Marcus confirmed.

"I burned your poem," I told her. "I memorized it first. Without the paper, the shirt never would have caught. Even then it only lasted a few minutes."

Marcus said, "I can't believe you lasted almost a week out there. I thought for sure Brill did you in. I thought he dumped your body in Old Railroad Lake."

My eyes closed and my teeth clamped down as a sickening wave of intense burning rolled though my foot. I smiled weakly through it. "Brill . . . I need to thank him."

They all acted shocked. "Thank him? Are you nuts?" Reece asked. "You should have heard what he said about you being gone! I was so mad that I slugged him with my crutch."

Marcus joked, "Great weapon. I gotta get me one of those." He shot Reece an approving glance. "And she looks so harmless. . . ."

I said, "I'll explain later about Brill. Long story." I suddenly sat up. "Lake . . . I forgot to tell you," I wheezed. "It's in the lake!"

"What's in the lake?" Rob asked.

I glanced at the door. The parents and the twins were outside talking to Reece's mom. I whispered, *"Soterion."*

Reece's eyes popped. "What?! The helmet's in the lake? How do you know?"

"Maybe the rest of it too." I held out my hand to Marcus. "Quella." He turned his over to me. I fell back to the pillow, punched in Deuteronomy 33:23, and handed it back.

His cool green eyes locked onto the screen. "Naphtali—"

"It means 'fighter,'" I interrupted.

He read silently, frowned, then said out loud, "Will inherit southward . . . to the lake."

"We gotta get it now," I said.

"But the lake's frozen!" Rob said.

The hallway crowd came back in, and we switched the conversation to how far behind I was in Latin and how long until I'd walk again. Rob joked that he'd be organizing a homecoming parade in my honor down Main Street.

As Reece stood to leave, I squeezed her hand and whispered, "We're not waiting until spring."

She nodded.

Chapter 12

THE doctor, a bald guy with bushy eyebrows and a wide smile, stood at the foot of my bed and discussed my situation with Mom and Dad. I'd insisted on it; I didn't want somebody sealing my fate out in the hallway and me not knowing about it.

According to the doctor, I was—in a nutshell—sort of a natural miracle. He said, "His foot was frostbitten for an entire week. But the conditions were—how shall I say this?—ideal, under the circumstances. He was wearing good shoes, the shoe stayed dry, he was out of the wind, and the collective heat from the rocks kept his foot a consistent temperature. When flesh freezes, thaws, and refreezes, you have serious problems, deep tissue damage. Apparently, that didn't happen here."

The whole Creek family knew this kind of stuff from first-aid classes. Mom and Dad looked at the doctor in pleasant disbelief.

"You're used to the cold?" he asked me.

"I hike barefoot sometimes."

The doctor smiled at his chart and then at me. "That's part of it too. You'd already acclimated. A person from the tropics would have . . . succumbed. I hear you had a top-notch sleeping bag; you're strong and healthy. Still, with the fluctuations in temperature over the past week, I fully expected permanent damage." He took one more look at the foot and touched it ever so slightly in a few places. "Hurts?"

"Like the dickens."

"We'll keep him a few more days; those toes aren't out of the woods yet—no pun intended—but healing is taking place." The doctor shook his head in wonder.

"People prayed for me," I said.

He looked at my parents and back at me. "I'll say. I'd have to consider the likelihood that *someone* was adjusting the thermostat in that gorge."

I smiled, closed my eyes, and nodded. The doctor was a believer.

When I'd been pumped with painkillers and left alone to rest, I drifted under a snow-white warm blanket and realized that I'd had exactly what I needed to survive: no more, no less. Not the bread and meat that I wanted, but good gear, three cups of water, and a steady temperature. And the Presence.

Reece came by the next day with a Christmas gift: a leather Bible and new batteries for the Quella. "I don't want you to ever be without the Word again. And don't be discouraged or afraid because of what happened, Elijah. Whatever Satan tried to do to you by trapping you back there, he didn't get away with it. He's not going to stop us."

"I'm . . . uh . . . I'm not sure it was him."

She sat back, stunned. "What do you mean?"

I explained how the rock fell, how my foot was protected all around, and what the doctor said. "It seemed that my foot never actually froze. So there's no permanent damage. I'll be more susceptible to frostbite from here on out. I know that, but I'll be good to go." I got quiet and didn't know how to say it. "I'm sorry everybody was worried. I feel bad about it. I was dumb to try moving that rock on my own. But—and I mean this, I'm not just talking—I'm glad it happened." I flipped through the Bible and smelled the leather and new-book smell. "Wow, this is awesome. It's small enough to fit right in my hand."

"You said reading the Bible helped."

"Oh, man . . . at our next powwow I'll tell you all what happened." I choked up thinking about it. "When I get home, we'll have an old movie and pizza night. I'll lay it all out. I'll write it down for Mei too. Reece, thanks for the Bible. I'm sorry I don't have anything for you."

"You can owe me." She grinned and poked me. "You're one of those last-minute shoppers, huh?"

"Yeah, that's it. I was waiting for the after-Christmas bargains."

Mom kept me on the living room couch to monitor me and keep me from trying to rush my recovery. She treated me like a prince. What kind of food did I want? Did I want to watch TV or read a book? Did I need it all quiet in the house to rest?

She helped me catch up on homework—only when I felt like it—and called in a Latin tutor. She even hired a masseuse to work the kinks out of my neck and back. Yeah, for a few days I was a prince.

On the front burner of my mind, though, was how to get to the bottom of Silver Lake. I was more than ready to get a scuba suit and dive down myself, but that would be dumb. Reece couldn't. So I called Rob. *"Soterion,"* I said. "What do we do about it?"

"The water temperature is thirty-eight degrees. The depth of the lake is fifteen feet in the middle."

"You measured it already?" I asked, amazed.

Rob was all business. "Dom has a wet suit, but not for icy waters. It might work though. Marcus said he'd fit in it."

I pictured Skidmore in a baggy diving suit dropping backward off Paddleboat Dock. "Deep-sea diving in Silver Lake. That's a hoot. Or hey, we could drain it."

"It would take a day and draw too much attention." Rob's take-charge attitude surprised me. I wondered if he'd been thinking about what to do if I'd turned up dead.

Funny, though, I wasn't offended or threatened or anything. It was a good thing. They would have gone on without me.

"Diving's the best idea," he said, as if that settled it. "Marcus said he'd try to clear it with his dad and get things set up. We're calling it Operation Naphtali."

"Okay, Cuz. You'll be in charge. Hey, by the way, do you know how Donovan got involved in my rescue?"

"Donovan was here?"

"Yeah. You didn't know?"

"No."

"He and Dom . . . the way they were talking during the rescue in Gilead. It was like they knew each other."

I was soon putting weight on the foot. I got a pile of get-well cards from school kids and teachers and church people. Mom was impressed and sort of baffled at how the church people brought food over even though they didn't know her. It was like when Reece was recovering. A ton of food just showed up.

I moved up to my room when I convinced Mom that I wasn't going to die or do something stupid with my recovery.

On the night of Operation Naphtali, Rob came over after dinner dressed all in black and wearing a stocking cap, like at Farr Island. He had the walkie-talkies and handed me one. "We're doing it now. You'll be able to hear what's going on. Marcus will actually do the retrieval; his dad's here to help. Your dad knows about it but signed off because he has a planning meeting. Dom has all this equipment: underwater lights, ropes, everything. I'll report in."

"Where will you look? It's a big lake."

He unfolded a map. "Here's the lake, and here's where Old Pilgrim Church stood. I'm starting with the assumption that Dowland came from the church, took the shortest path to the lake, and hurled it toward the center. I drew a straight line to show direction. Marcus will start from this point on the shore and work his way toward the center. You'll hear from me in a few minutes, Navajo." He turned to leave but then turned back. "I ordered myself one of those Quellas."

I was totally impressed with my cousin. I hated missing the eyewitness action, but the search couldn't have been in better hands.

I lay in my bed and prayed, "Let them find it quick. It's cold out there, and Marcus is a city boy from the tropics."

In a few minutes, Rob called in. "Viking to Navajo. Out."

I grinned. "Navajo here. Out."

"Cong here," Marcus's voice came through the walkie-talkie with splashing in the background.

"Metatron here," came Dom's booming, overly dramatic voice. I laughed out loud. *Metatron. Come on.*

"Little Soaring Eagle here." It was Reece.

"Going in," said Marcus, and I heard a big splash.

Rob's voice came through. "Operation Naphtali underway. I'll report back in a few minutes. Over and out."

I lay there with the walkie-talkie on my chest, more glad to be alive than I could put in words. *Thank you, El-Telan-Yah. Thank you, thank you, thank you.* I lay there, a big squishy pile of gratitude, sensing a cloud of goodness around me.

After a few minutes, the walkie-talkie crackled. "Viking here. Status report. Cong is nearing the center of the lake. No retrieval at this point."

"He's been under for ten minutes, right? Over."

"Nine minutes, thirty seconds."

"Don't let him get too cold. He's a tropical guy, you know. Can't handle the winter temps the way we Ohioans can."

"We're monitoring him. Viking over and out."

"Navajo over and out," I said, grinning from ear to ear.

I could hardly contain myself. I sat up and eased my still puffy, blistery foot onto the floor. I threw on my jacket, wrapped my foot in a T-shirt, got the walkie-talkie, and eased down the stairs on my backside. At the foot of the stairs, I stood. "Mom, I'm stepping out on the porch for just a minute."

She came running. "Oh, hon! No, it's too soon."

"For just a minute. I've been cooped up for days. See, it's much better. Rob's down by the lake. We're using the walkie-talkies. I want to wave at him."

Reluctantly she went back to the kitchen. "Five minutes . . . and keep that foot covered."

I stepped out on the porch in the dark. It was an eerie sight, two guys and a girl all in black, looking over the lake while a faint green light moved slowly through its depths.

"Navajo here," I spoke into the walkie-talkie. "I'm on the porch. Status."

Rob and Reece turned and waved. "Viking and Little Soaring Eagle here. He's been out to the center once. Working his way back. It's very murky. Out."

I went back in so I wouldn't worry Mom but stayed in the front room and sat by the window, peeking through the curtain every minute or so. She brought me some hot chocolate. I'd felt a weird kind of guilty, hiding the good news from my mom. I had to tell her. *It's now or never.*

"Mom?"

"What do you need, hon?"

"Um, Marcus is in the lake."

She looked at me like I'd lost my mind.

"He's searching for another piece of the armor."

She dashed to the window, took one look down toward the lake, and gasped.

Before she could blow a gasket, I said, "Dom's overseeing the operation. Reece and Rob are there. And Dad knows."

She whirled around. At first she didn't believe me. Then hurt feelings showed up on her face. "Your dad gave you permission?"

"Mom, I got a revelation when I was stuck in the gorge. A verse from the Bible made me think that the last pieces might be in the lake. They might not, but we have to look."

Glaring down toward the lake, Mom did a slow burn. She had never understood what the quest was about. She couldn't see the big picture. I was puzzling over how to explain it when my eyes fell on the Christmas bears and angels sitting on the couch. I hobbled over and picked them up. "Okay, here it is. Here's why the search is important. These are real, Mom. Bears are real. And *angels* are real. We have angels at Christmas because angels came. The spirit world is as real as the real world, Mom."

"Honey, I don't deny that there could be something out there, life on other planets . . ."

"I'm not talking aliens or some *things* out there! I mean God and demons and angelic forces." I held up a bear in coveralls and an angel in a pretty satin dress. "This is a big joke, Mom. In real life both of these beings can use deadly force against you."

You'd have thought I was a preschooler talking about my imaginary friends. It wasn't sinking in. My mom seemed like a stranger to me.

The dryer buzzed. "The laundry's done," she said, obviously relieved for an excuse to end the conversation. I had one more thing to say. It was more good news, but she wasn't going to like it.

"Mom, remember that song they sang at my baptism about me never being the same?"

"Yes, I think so."

"Well, that's true—and it's getting truer by the minute."

She left me holding a half-empty cup of hot chocolate and with a worrisome question on my mind: Which was worse, to worship the sun the way Mei did, or to believe in nothing, like Mom? I was working on it in my mind when the walkie-talkie crackled and Viking blurted, "We have the arm piece!"

Chapter 13

IT took a few more minutes for Marcus to find the helmet. I stood out in the driveway—my foot bundled in the T-shirt, the walkie-talkie pressed to my mouth. "Navajo to Viking. Bring it to the house. I told Mom. All's clear. Over."

We clan members beamed over the pond-scummy helmet wrapped in soggy burlap. Mom studied it with the strangest expression. "Now . . . just how did you know this was in our lake?"

I grinned. "God told me."

She looked worried.

Dom thawed out in the kitchen and tried to explain things to Mom. I was glad for the help.

"No sign of the sword, I guess," I asked Marcus as the four of us clunked and thudded up the steps.

"I looked."

Reece, Marcus, and I crowded around Rob in the bathroom while he washed the arm piece and helmet in the tub. Dr. Dale's comments came back to me, about how unready we were for what was to come after the quest. I could still hear the half-scared, half-angry tone in the old scientist's voice: "*. . . Rob's disbelief, Sahara's pagan influence over Mei, Reece's health, Marcus's ego, and your lack of understanding* *of the simplest truths of the faith. You five are completely unprepared for the task ahead. Not one of you has the vaguest idea what kind of spiritual and physical danger you are in."*

From where I sat—on the bathroom floor, wedged between the toilet and the tub—we sure didn't look like spiritual warriors: me with my breadbasket-size foot, Reece with her crutch, Rob dressed like a ninja, and Marcus shivering in shorts and T-shirt. We looked like the Magdeline chapter of Rejects Anonymous.

Once Rob got the scum washed off the helmet, it gleamed. My heart warmed at seeing that gold-tinted relic again with the mysterious symbols carved into the forehead.

Reece took a towel and swaddled the arm piece like a baby. Rubbing the metal forearm until the word appeared, she whispered, *"Koinonia.* Fellowship." She took the helmet and said with emotion, *"Soterion.* Salvation." She grinned big at Marcus and me. "We have to tell Mei!"

Rob said, "I've been reading up on these words. They're written in an early form of the Greek alphabet—except for that." He pointed to the second letter on the helmet. "It's the omega, the big *O* which was added later. It's now the last letter of the Greek alphabet. It means 'the end.'"

Marcus said, "Jesus called himself the alpha and the omega. The beginning and the end."

Reece ran her finger over the omega symbol Ω, hugged the helmet, then handed it to me. "You keep it for a while. Your room will be headquarters until you're better."

We took the pieces to my room and then went down to the kitchen to thank Dom for helping us. When the others left, I went to my room, turned on my bedside lamp, and propped myself up to study the helmet and arm piece. Things I hadn't understood before were clear to me now. *Soterion* meant a person's soul saved, not a soldier's life saved. The winding vine and spikes were Jesus' crown of thorns; the reddish dots were his blood. I went to sleep with the helmet and arm piece next to me and thought about the stories hidden in the armor.

I woke while it was still dark, clicked on the light, and lay there full of wonder studying the helmet inch by inch. *Why did you choose me?* I asked God.

The inside of the helmet was worn and ragged and still damp. In the strong lamplight, I noticed that the high inside part of the metal nosepiece wasn't metal at all. It was soft. I pressed in with my thumb. *It's like clay but with a thin coat of metallic paint over it.* Pressing around the spot revealed nubs of what looked like tiny fasteners that had broken off. I sat up, held it under the lamp, and looked closer. A small square piece of something had once been fastened to the inside of the nosepiece and had fallen off. It had to be the little scrap of chain mail with an encryption of Job 22:25: "Then the Almighty will be your gold, the choicest silver for you."

Dr. Eloise had explained that the Hebrew word for *gold*

in that verse referred to metal in a crude state, or "dug out," as in a treasure uncovered. "The root word also carries the idea of defense," she had said. "It may be translated *gold,* or *treasure,* or *defense.* And it looks like you children have found all three!"

Something hard was embedded in the layer of clay. Using the tip of my bowie knife, I carefully dug out a red stone—a crystal or a garnet maybe. It was large—obviously not a real jewel—and shaped like a raindrop. I hobbled to the bathroom and washed it off, careful not to let it slip down the drain.

When I held it to the bathroom light, I saw that it was a pure bloodred. And though I'm not a jewelry kind of guy, I thought it was beautiful. It was cut with little triangle facets all around. *Looks like a piece off a chandelier or an old lamp. Wonder what it's worth?*

Mom had errands to run the next day and insisted I come along. I wasn't anxious to be gaped at and asked questions about my condition, but Mom had finally noticed that my winter jacket was two sizes too small, and she wanted to fit me in a new one. I was to sit in the car while she went to the drugstore for my anti-infection medicine.

Across the street—where the old hotel had once stood before the tornado ripped through—was a barber shop and the recently opened New York Jewelers, both with apartments above. I had the gem in my pocket.

Chapter 13

Wonder what it's worth? It's probably a piece of glass symbolizing the blood of Jesus, and they'll probably laugh at me. Could be a ruby or a garnet. What if they thought I stole it? I could lie and say it was a family heirloom. No. I sat in the car gazing across the street at a sign in the window: "Introductory Offer! Free Appraisals!" Behind the counter stood a man in his forties, clean-cut, wearing a business suit. *Rob's been doing research. My turn.*

I got out of the car and hobbled across the street. The door jingled as I went in; the salesman looked up. "Good morning," he said, straightening the ring trays and locking the case.

"Hi. Do you do appraisals?"

He nodded to the sign and looked at me as if I didn't have the sense God gave a duck.

"Oh." I pulled the stone out and laid it on the counter. "Is this worth anything? It came out of an old piece. Belongs to the clan."

"Clan?" He smiled coolly and asked in a northern accent, "That's what you call family around here?" He took the stone in his fingers and put a jeweler's loupe to his eye. "Let's have a look."

He turned it in his hand. Then he turned it over and looked some more. His cool, big-city smirk faded to a look of confusion. He leaned down, his eyes seriously boring into the gem. He stopped breathing. I got uneasy. He suddenly seemed aware that I was watching him and tried to recover his air of casualness. "Very pretty stone. Old." He looked me over and then went back to the stone as if he hadn't believed his eyes the first time. "Are you . . . interested in selling it?"

"What's it worth? I mean, is it glass or a ruby or what?"

"It's not glass," he said cautiously. He was so stunned by the gem that I half expected him to tell me it was engraved with words or symbols. *Why hadn't I thought of that before? I should have looked closer, should have left the research part to Rob. Drat!*

"It's . . . valuable," he said matter-of-factly. "You said you found it with other pieces of jewelry? Is the jewelry your mother's or grandmother's?" He was gathering information.

I wished I hadn't come, wished I hadn't let a stranger see it. *What were you thinking, Creek? It's from the armor of God! You never underestimate it. Haven't you learned anything?*

I took a cue from the Stallards' wheeling and dealing with Cravens in Dublin a few months before. *Okay,* I coached myself, *you came in here with one question, and you're going out with one answer. Simple as that.* "You said free appraisals." I nodded to the sign.

"Yes, appraisals." He studied the stone again. "It's an older cut, called a briolette. A style from—" he cleared his throat, "older times. A simple cut like this doesn't provide the refraction of newer, better cuts. We could have it reshaped for you."

Oh, so now it's inferior? Sorry, bud, I just watched you lose your cool over that stone. "Is it a garnet?"

"Possibly a corundum."

"What's that?"

His eyes went all wide and innocent. "A harder stone. I'll need to confirm the age before I can give you an informed appraisal." He nodded to the back room. "Would you mind if I showed this to my associate?"

A wave of panic washed over me. I was no idiot. He was planning to go back there, find a substitute gem, and do the old switcheroo. I held out my hand. "I just wanted to know what it's worth, ballpark figure. Free appraisal and all that."

He balked. "All right. Value. I could . . . offer you five hundred dollars."

"Is that what it's worth?"

He faltered. "Maybe seven-fifty. It has a few flaws, but the color is very nice."

"What did you say it was?"

"It's a—" Sweat popped out on his face. "It appears to be a diamond, but the cut is unusual. It's an older cut."

"You said that."

He nodded toward the back again. "So I'd like to confer with my associate to give you a more informed answer. If he concurs, we could do, say . . . a thousand."

I looked at the gem, glistening bloodred between his shaking fingers. "Diamonds aren't red," I said.

"Red ones are relatively rare," he said casually. He licked his lips; his mouth was dry.

Thinks he can pull one over on the dumb small-town kid. I faked total shock. "Whoa, did you say a thousand *whole dollars!*" This guy didn't know who he was dealing with. I had international connections, friends on the police force and in the world of science. I had all but the last piece of the armor of God. "Well, thanks. That's really neat to know! A thousand dollars . . . wow!"

"Or more, if I might show it to my associate. Then if you decide to keep it, we could put it in a nice setting for you."

Yeah, right. "You could?" I asked in a dumb, gawky way. "Could you put it in . . . like a silver dragon head with the red diamond as the eye or something?"

"Sure, sure, we could do that for you," he said with an agreeable frown, as if he were thinking out how to do it. "A striking idea."

He thinks I'm dumb and *have no taste?!* Well, to give him a little credit here, I hadn't actually combed my hair that morning. I was wearing a coat with sleeves halfway to my elbows, old sandals, and two pairs of big, fluffy white socks to pad my feet.

I kept my hand out and added a country twang, thinking how Rob might do it: "Welp, I'll think 'bout that dragon head with a big red eye on a big silver chain around my neck. That'd be nice. Real nice."

Reluctantly he dropped the diamond into my palm and followed it with a business card. "Our designers can set the stone according to your specifications—a dragon or a magnificent brooch to surprise your mother on her birthday. As a first-time customer, you'll receive an extra twenty percent discount on the setting. Now if you'll just fill out this card, we'll put you on our mailing list."

"Maybe later. I need to think 'bout that."

"We do appreciate your business. You live in town?"

I limped toward the door, bouncing in my springy white socks. "Family's from down in Georgia."

"It was certainly nice to meet you . . . ," he fished for my name.

"Known 'round some parts as George Telanoo."

Once out of view, I jogged painfully down the street. I wasn't about to get in Mom's car and have him trace our license plate. *This was a huge mistake. Huge. Why did he want that stone so stinking bad? Why would he lie and call it a red diamond? There's no such thing!*

I glanced back when I reached the corner. He'd come out of the store and was watching me. I saluted him with my index finger, ducked into a side alley, and thought fast. *The treasure? Dowland's lost treasure?*

I had to get to the car before Mom found me missing. I circled around the backside of the block, cut through the parking lot next to the tracks, and limped back up another alley. I peeked around the corner. The jeweler had gone inside. I watched for Mom to come out of the drugstore and waved for her to come pick me up.

"What are you doing on your feet, Elijah? It's freezing!"

"Can you drop me off at Rob's?"

"Absolutely not! It's back home to rest. You have to get healed before school starts!" She patted my knee and mellowed. "You're a little stir-crazy; after what you've been through, I don't blame you. We'll invite Rob over when we get home."

"Wait. Drop me off here at the library."

Mom groaned impatiently. "Elijah!"

"I have to!!"

She pulled up to the curb.

"Thanks, Mom. I'll be an hour. I'll call if I need a ride."

"Don't you dare try to walk home!"

I called Rob on the library's pay phone and kept my voice down so the ever-suspicious Mrs. Otto wouldn't hear. "Can you get to the library?"

"Yeah. What's up?"

"I don't know, could be big. Bring paper and pencil. We'll need to take notes."

"Are you trying to get me to do your homework?" he asked skeptically.

"No, jerk. Make it snappy."

Chapter 14

WE found the most out-of-the-way table in the library, and I laid the gem on a piece of white paper. "It was in the helmet. Right behind the nosepiece in a lump of clay that had been painted to look like metal. Right here." I pointed to my forehead. I told him about the jeweler's reaction. "I think it's worth a lot! We're not telling another soul, not even Reece or Marcus. Not yet."

Rob grabbed every book on gems he could find, careful not to arouse Mrs. Otto's wary lemur eyes. I kept watch on the door through the bookshelves, wondering if the jeweler had spied on me from a back window in his shop; I wondered if he was flipping through the phone book looking for Telanoo. I'd never be able to walk down the streets of Magdeline again, at least not past New York Jewelers. I imagined him keeping a camera handy, snapping my mug, and flashing it around town until he'd tracked me down. *Oh no!* The Magdeline Messenger! *The story of the missing boy—me—was on the front page last week! Would a big-city jeweler bother reading a podunk town paper? Will he think I found the gem behind the camp? Will he call in his big-city hit men, who'll break into Camp Mudj and hold my family hostage until I turn over the stone?*

I'd become high profile in my own town, and I didn't like the feel of it. Not one bit.

Rob rifled through books, slamming each one shut when it didn't deliver the information he wanted. In a few minutes, he shoved a book at me with pictures of gemstones. "Red diamonds. They do exist, but they're very, *very* rare! Found first in India, then Australia, and often called pinks because they aren't a true red."

I held my gem up to the light. "This one is."

He peered up at it, then pulled the book back under his nose, and read on: "Some have an orange or brown cast . . . it doesn't say anything about a pure red diamond . . . no wait . . . it says here, 'No true red diamond has ever been catalogued.'"

I locked eyes with my cousin. "Notice it didn't say never discovered, just never catalogued."

We took turns holding it to the light and keeping an eye out for Mrs. Otto or any library people. I whispered, "Maybe this is the only one in the world; diamond experts know it's out there but not *where.*" My mind flashed back to Grafton Institute in Dublin and how Cravens had paced like a caged animal at feeding time when the subject of the armor of God came up. I looked at Rob. "What did Cravens say? Something like, 'No man can own it'?"

"'A treasure of immeasurable wealth,'" Rob quoted. "'No man can purchase it, for it cannot be appraised.'"

"Did he mean the diamond or the armor?" I asked.

"Do you think the Stallards know?" Rob wondered out loud.

"If they did, why didn't they tell us?"

Mrs. Otto came tromping around on her way to the periodicals. I slipped the diamond into my pocket.

"Maybe this is what the Stallards have really been looking for all along," I said, trying not to sound suspicious.

"Do we have to tell them we found it?" he asked.

The Stallards had done so much for us. But in the light of our new discovery, my old suspicions returned. Why had they spent thousands on us?

Reluctantly I said, "I think we have to tell them about the helmet. But maybe not the diamond."

"Where will we hide it?"

I felt to make sure the diamond hadn't fallen out through a hole in my raggedy jacket. "Not in any of our houses; our moms might find it when they clean."

"Not out in the woods," he began, and I butted in before he said it, "where I lost the helmet once. I won't lose another treasure. That's all we need to say about that." I practically broke out in a cold sweat thinking about how last night I'd washed off the diamond over an open drain.

"Where are we going to hide it?" Rob repeated.

"Where am *I* going to hide it," I corrected.

"Elijah!" he hissed. "Don't start that again! It belongs to all of us! You can't take it!"

"The fewer who know, the better. Rob, you didn't see the hungry look in the eye of that jeweler. If news gets out, it could be dangerous."

Mrs. Otto's hot breath swept down on my neck.

I looked around; she was hovering. "May I help you gentlemen?" she fired at us.

"We're sorry for being loud," I whispered. "We'll get quiet and work on our research."

"Did I overhear one of you talking about taking something, because as a point of interest, there's been a rash of stealing from the library," she said accusingly.

"We're not stealing, Mrs. Otto," Rob said politely.

"And for that reason," she went on as if she hadn't heard, "a security guard comes by periodically to do random searches on suspicious patrons."

A search? The red diamond's not even safe in my raggedy old pocket in the town library!?

"We're legit," I said politely.

After she tromped off, Rob whispered, "So where?"

"I'll tell you Monday when I figure it out."

He gave me a look.

"I have to think."

Rob and I parted ways. He took off for home. I flagged down Bo in the camp van on a run to the hardware store. *Where? Where can I hide it?* By the time I reached the Camp Mudj maintenance building, I had the answer. It was the only possible place. I slipped in the door, went to the cabinet where we keep fasteners, ripped off a piece of duct tape, and sealed the diamond in my belly button.

Rob was at my locker first thing.

"Where'd you hide it?"

"Where no one will find it."

He snorted like a bull. "More than one person has to know."

Mysteriously I answered, "It's at the source of life and nourishment."

He thought about it a minute. "You gave it to your MOM?!"

I glanced down the hall. The coast was clear. I pointed to my navel. "You know, umbilical cord."

He made a face. "How'd you—?"

"Duct tape."

"That stuff will rot your skin after a while."

"It's not a permanent solution. But I can't leave it lying around, can't bury it, and can't hide it in the woods. There's no other place."

He giggled. "Hope you don't lose it in all that belly button lint. Hey, you could get a safety deposit box at the bank."

"I don't trust the bank."

"Don't go paranoid on us," he snapped, which was funny coming from my once scaredy-cat cousin. "What do we do about Marcus and Reece?"

I thought a minute. "We show them but don't tell where it'll be hidden. The only reason I'm telling you is in case somebody kills me. If that happens, you get to the morgue first and rip it out."

"You're retarded," he scowled. "That's not going to happen. You're just talking morbid 'cause you—"

"'Cause I almost died and got my bones picked clean by owls and ravens and coyotes? Yeah. It changes you, man. It changes you."

Mom got past her compulsion to hover over me every single minute, so Dad dragged her out to dinner and a movie. Nothing had been said about Isabel MacMerrit in a while, which was okay with me. I had enough on my mind.

The clan gathered for a powwow around the fire in our family room. For them it was business as usual. But after the week in Gilead, I saw my clan in a whole new light: hanging out with them was pure gold. I had three surprises for Reece, all in ring boxes. I handed her the first. She gave me a weird, embarrassed, half-mad look. The guys grinned.

"What's this?" she scowled and turned red. Then she opened it and broke into a big smile.

"It's a Trinity ring," I explained. "The three interlocking rings represent Father, Son, and Holy Spirit. It has a double meaning for the clan: a cord of three strands is not quickly broken. Late Christmas present."

She tried it on, stretched out her hand to show it off, and beamed. Then, just to pay me back for putting her on the spot, she kissed me right on the mouth in front of the guys. They hollered, "Woohoo!" and "Yeehaw!" and acted like idiots. I went red and handed her the next box. It had the same thing in it: a Trinity ring. "This is from us three guys for Mei. You can send it to her as a reminder that we haven't forgotten her."

She bubbled over and hugged us all.

I handed her the third box. "This is a gift from the armor to all of us. Marcus hasn't seen it either, but I'll let you open it."

She carefully popped open the lid. Lying on a little cushion of satin was the perfect, raindrop-shaped red stone. She touched it with the tip of her finger. "What is it?"

"It's a red diamond," I said soberly. "Maybe the only pure red diamond ever to exist. I found it in a little secret compartment in the nosepiece of the helmet."

We took turns looking at the gem close up in the firelight.

"You're sure it's a diamond?" Marcus asked.

"That's what the jeweler said. It's got to be worth a bundle. But here's the downside: the guy practically groveled to buy it from me, kept going up on the price, insisting that he had to take it into the back room and consult with his associate about it." I nodded knowingly. "He was trying to pull the old switcheroo."

Marcus leaned in to me, glaring. "You showed it to somebody? A piece of the armor?! Man, this is a monster problem!"

"I know that! I'm sorry! But look at it; would you think it's a diamond? All the diamonds I've ever seen are white and shaped like . . . diamonds!"

Rob defended me. "He didn't know red ones existed. Did *you?*"

Marcus shrugged. "No."

I said, "First question: do we tell the Stallards?"

We discussed it a long time and couldn't come to a conclusion. The old archaeologists had given us free reign with the armor, trusting us with its secrets. But around the fire and with lots of quiet time between words, we each admitted that in the backs of our minds, we'd all questioned their motives. Weird as they were, the Stallards seemed too good to be true. (It did occur to me once that they might not even be from this earth, but I chalked that crazy idea up to my recent encounters with the dark side of the spirit world, which can grab onto a person's imagination and not let go.)

Reece said thoughtfully, "After that day at Grafton Institute, they were more nervous than ever about news of the armor leaking out."

Rob added worriedly, "The high-powered recording devices and binoculars, how they could track down Francine when the police couldn't even find her . . . they're not the crusty old professors we first thought."

"I hate to say this," I concluded, "but we need another opinion." I turned to Marcus. "Hey, is your dad friends with Donovan?"

"The friend of the Stallards? Not that I know of."

"He and your dad were both at the gorge when they

rescued me. They talked a long time in private, but once I got to the hospital, I never saw Donovan again."

Marcus thought long and hard. "Dad never told me they knew each other, but . . ." He sat up, intrigued. "Remember the night we went on maneuvers to find the breastplate, that night down by the tracks? I was curious why our parents agreed to let a total stranger lead us on that operation. Didn't that seem bizarre?"

I shrugged, "I was so antsy that I didn't care. What I'm getting at is this: if your dad knows Donovan who knows the Stallards, and your dad knows the Stallards from years back . . ."

Rob said, "We should ask your dad about them."

I added, "We don't have to show him the diamond."

I was surprised that Dom Skidmore would drop everything and come right over. When he joined our circle in the glowing firelight, I got flashbacks of Farr Island and half expected another ghost story. We reminded him that we had all but one piece of the armor and were pretty sure that the whole thing was going to turn out to be valuable. We asked if he had the inside scoop on the Stallards and if they could be trusted.

He looked absently around the room like he was thinking hard. Then he put his hands on his thighs and blew out a big, decisive breath. He squinted briefly at me and barked, "Okay! Here it is. Point one: back during World War II—

which was called the war to end all wars, but didn't—there was an archaeologist named Nelson Glueck. While war raged around the world, Glueck continued his work—in the interest of science, you see. The enemy didn't quite grasp that archaeologists have precise knowledge of landscape. And they dig. *They dig!* Caves and tunnels."

He gave us a few minutes to think about that.

"In that war—right under the noses of the enemy and with the full knowledge and cooperation of Allied Intelligence—secret escapes were being prepared in case things went bad and the troops had to flee." He sat back and let it sink in some more. I was drawing a blank. What did this have to do with the Stallards?

Rob's eyes got wide. "Archaeologists on secret missions for the government?"

Dom smiled. "More was at stake than a military victory in those days. If the Allied Forces had failed their mission, we might all be living under the iron fist of global oppression: death camps, firing squads, perverse medical experiments. Point two: throughout history, when persecution of the church is on the rise, people go underground. I don't necessarily mean under the ground as in cellars and caves. It could be in a small group around a dinner table, or sitting by the fire in a nice house on a cold winter evening." He winked at me. "Or in handmade shelters in remote natural hideouts. As we speak, tens of millions of Christians are worshiping God underground."

Rob began, "Are you saying—"

Dom shot him a look. "I'm not saying a thing. All I'm saying is that archaeologists are allowed into areas—even war zones or hostile countries—to do research and rescue antiquities. I'm saying archaeologists know where ancient tombs are. Caves. Tunnels."

Rob asked again, "So are you telling us that—"

"I'm not telling you a thing. All I'm saying is that the war to end all wars didn't. But one is coming that will. Armageddon. Things are heating up for it—people's faith being tried, their rights slipping through their fingers— subtle and slow. Today in The Window, some folks have no freedom at all, and death is sure if they speak the name of Jesus. The Window will widen; more and more believers will have to make difficult decisions: 'Do I hide? Do I preach the Word and run? Do I take a stand and die? Or do I play the coward, keep my trap shut? Do I wait for the heat to die down?'" He shrugged.

"Hide where?" Reece asked.

He leaned forward, "Where *in the world?*"

Rob rolled his eyes at me, and I knew what he was thinking: *Dominic Skidmore, long on questions, short on answers.* I was sort of getting on his wavelength, though, and saw how you can pass on information by asking really good questions.

"Wait a minute!" Rob cried, looking around at us, his blue eyes wide and wondering. "Newgrange passage tomb! The forbidden tunnel under Dunluce Castle where the Stallards went because they had," he made air quotes, "clearance!"

Reece said excitedly, "There were other tombs at Newgrange. Unexcavated tombs the Stallards knew all about." She asked Dom, "Do you mean that the Stallards are making hiding places all over the world for the Day of Evil?"

Dom threw up his hands. "You didn't hear it from me."

I fell back on the couch, dumbstruck. "They were showing us around! Newgrange, Dunluce, the Christian retreat house in Belfast. They were giving us a tour! So are you saying their archaeology projects are all a front, a way to get into places and make caves and tunnels where people can preach all over the world and then disappear when the Day of Evil comes?"

Dom smiled. "Did *I* say that? I *never* said that!" He leaned back, locking his hands behind his head. "The big picture, people, has always been about saving the world."

I sat bolt upright again. "Wait a minute! Saving the world? Hold on! Yancy and Peck, the guys who played the boo hags at Farr Island. When we visited the base, Peck signed off saying, 'Gotta get back to saving the world.' What did he mean by that? He wasn't talking military?"

Dom gave me a friendly fist in the arm. "I just can't say, Creek. I just can't say."

Rob asked excitedly, "Are there hiding places around

here? And who's Donovan? What part does he play in all this?"

Dom started to make a comment but stopped and took a hard look at Rob. "You're not a believer, are you, Viking?"

Rob's mouth dropped open, he stammered, then cried in a singsong voice, "Uh-huuuh! I belieeeeve!"

Dom raised a cool eyebrow and looked in that instant just like his son. "Haven't made it public, Viking. Haven't claimed the name. Haven't joined up. No, sir, I haven't seen your sins floating around in the watery grave of a baptistery." He went eyeball to eyeball with Rob. "Wingate, I got no proof at all of your allegiance to the cause. None. From where I sit, you've been coasting. So in answer to your many questions—" Dom tapped Rob's chin with his knuckle, "I could let you in on the whole secret plan, give you names, addresses, show you the global grid. I could do that, Viking," he said with threat in every muscle, "but then I'd have to kill you."

Chapter 15

THAT death threat from Dom Skidmore was all Rob
needed. We were at church the next Sunday. Rob told on
himself to his parents and mine about the rubber ducky
caper so I couldn't give him payback during his baptism.
I was so looking forward to dropping some big animal in
on him and causing a sensation that would make church
history, but it wasn't to be. When he stepped down into the
baptistery, Marcus and I yelled, "Go, Ballyrob!"

With a swelling in my heart, I sat on the third pew with
the youth group and watched my cousin claim the name
and go under. *Four of my clan of five are in. One to go: Mei. All
of the pieces found but the last. One to go.*

I was called in to the principal's office first thing Monday.
My mind spun. *What kind of trouble am I in now? Detention for
the masked ball incident? Is Abner on a rampage because I whiled
away the hours facedown and dying under a two-ton rock in the gorge
when I could have been working on Latin declensions?*

Mr. Erwin was middle-aged with a round, ruddy face and
manicured hands, a soft-spoken guy who had the respect
of the students because he was the real McCoy. Nice but
tough. He was wearing a light yellow shirt with a navy tie
and gold cuff links. He had me sit in the big chair across

from his desk, the seat often warmed by many an innocent Latin student and more often by the big, guilty behinds of the Brill brothers.

"We're so glad you're all right, Elijah," he began. "Everyone was worried about you. When a young person disappears nowadays, the way things are in the world . . . well, we're all thankful it turned out well. I would like you to speak briefly to the student body before the pep rally today. We meant to have your father come last year and speak on this issue of survival, but regrettably didn't get to it. It's a near miracle you survived, and I think the students may be more likely to listen to an actual story. You've fully recovered?"

My words came out in a rush. "Yeah, I'm fine but the whole school?!"

He tapped a pencil on his desk good-naturedly. "A few minutes is all we want, Elijah. We'd like to present you with an award as well."

"Today?"

"Waiting will only make you more nervous. That's been my experience."

"What do I say?"

"Tell us how you survived, the tools and techniques you used. A few pointers."

"Thanks, but I'm not very good at public speaking. I'm taking speech next year though." I hoped he'd take the hint.

My man-of-action-not-of-words argument didn't cut

any slack with Mr. Erwin. By the time I got back to class, I was a wreck. *Me? Speak in front of the whole school!* At lunch I stopped Marcus in the hallway, looking for moral support. He listened and laughed. "You get an award for lying under a rock for a week? Nice work," and turned to saunter off.

It was just what I needed to hear. "Yeah, no big deal, huh? Crack a few jokes." I gulped hard.

He sauntered back to me and leaned in secretively. "You still don't get it, do you, Creek? You're the leader. So lead."

The day whizzed by. I couldn't concentrate. I got a note on my locker in Reece's handwriting: *You'll be great. Knock 'em dead!* I felt sick to my stomach.

All of Magdeline Independent filed into the gym and filled the bleachers. It felt like a public execution. Mom and Dad were there to see me get a citizenship award. I could hardly breathe. The principal stood behind the mike and said something, but I didn't hear a word until my name came up, ". . . our own Elijah Creek. Give him your full attention. His trial could one day save your life."

Dazed, I walked to the mike. "Shelter is the first priority," I said in the same way that I had begun dozens of camp classes before. Somehow this was different. My throat went dry. "You can live a week or more without water, a month without food. But in the cold, you have to have shelter. Preferably not a two-ton rock lying on top of you."

They laughed, and I relaxed a little. I explained what

shelter I did have: the cliff, an excellent sleeping bag, and the slab, which had both trapped me and stored the heat and, in the end, saved my foot. "I'm standing here today in spite of that rock and because of that rock."

Reece applauded. Her Devo club and a smattering of others followed suit.

"And you need water." I told about how I didn't have water because the canteen was out of reach, how the icicle had formed and melted in a matter of hours. "And fire. Fire is everything: it heats, cooks, sterilizes, lights the dark, keeps wild animals away." I paused. "I saved what little fire I had until the last minute, which was a good thing. The copter might never have spotted me otherwise. I'd been saving it for sterilizing the knife. If no one came by that next morning, I'd decided to use my belt as a tourniquet and amputate my leg."

The crowd had been half attentive until that moment. They went stone still.

"I planned to wait until the temperature was below freezing and I was not in the sun before cutting off my leg. I would have tightened the belt to keep from bleeding to death, and then exposed the stump to ice to freeze the blood to crystals and hopefully stop the flow. Then if I had any fire left, I would have seared the stump to cauterize the arteries. Then I would have crawled home."

Mom's hand clutched her stomach. Dad looked stricken and proud at the same time. All eyes—even Justin Brill's gang—were locked on me. And suddenly I wasn't afraid. I looked at Reece. She nodded as if to say, *Go on.*

I took the mike off the stand and walked along the bleachers. "But that's how my body survived. It's also important to know how to keep your mind from going stark raving mad alone in the dark; you need to know how not to let the fear swallow you whole out there in the wild. I'm telling you here and now to appreciate your families. Appreciate your blankets and chairs and running water and full refrigerators. They're luxuries a lot of people don't have."

I paced. "Coyotes were closing in on the last day, and I discovered that a nest of blue racer snakes was above my head in the cliff. I don't know how many: fifteen, thirty, a hundred."

A groan of repulsion went up from the crowd.

"One slithered down the tree to check me out but then disappeared. I had a hard time sleeping that night. To sum up, you need a fire kit, good shoes, a stash of food and water, a flashlight—because the darkness is horrible—and some kind of shelter, and this." I pulled the Quella from my pocket and held it up for the crowd to see. "I'll never go anywhere without this again. Anyone know what it is?"

Pitiful few hands went up: Marcus, Rob, Reece, and few from her Devo club. I walked the length of the gym in front of the bleachers, holding up the Quella. "It's the Word of God."

Most looked confused. A few teachers squirmed

uncomfortably. Justin's bunch muttered. Mom and Dad smiled uneasily. Mr. Erwin put his hand on the bleacher like he was ready to spring up and put an end to my speech. I walked back to the mike stand. "If that helicopter hadn't spotted me, I probably would have bled to death trying to get home, even with my outdoor skills. Sometimes you just don't make it. But my soul would have made it. Because of this."

You could have heard a pin drop.

"And prayer. Every day at roughly 3:00 a strange calm settled over me. I didn't know until later that my friends gathered every day at that time to pray for me. I felt it. You may not believe me, but it's true; I felt it." I put the mike back on the stand. "There's more to survival than just staying alive."

Electricity coursed through me, energizing and calming me as I sat down. A knot of emotion formed in my throat. I'd just preached a sermon.

I could tell by the look on Mr. Erwin's face that I hadn't given him what he wanted. But I didn't care. He made me get up again and handed me a certificate, and everyone clapped. A few even cheered for me.

The crowd transitioned to the pep rally once the cheerleaders took over; but I wasn't into it. I was thinking about the street preacher in Dublin and how he'd taught me to preach without even knowing it. Sitting there surrounded by screaming students, I realized it was probably my last chance to preach to the whole school. I wished I'd said more.

As we filed out for homeroom, a few people stopped me and wanted to see the Quella. Some said stuff like, "Good job!" and "Glad you made it, Elijah." Brill was lumbering on ahead. I slipped through the crowd and tapped him on the shoulder.

He turned. "Well if it isn't Nature Boy, crawling out from under his rock."

"Hey, Justin, I wanted to apologize for the incident at the dance. But, um . . . you don't talk about women that way, not in front of me anyhow." I reached out to shake his hand. He didn't respond, eyeing me darkly as usual. But this time I could see behind the dark to a kind of angry curiosity. I half smiled. "One more thing. I didn't mention it in there, but I found out something really interesting while I was trapped out in the wilderness: you sound a lot like Satan. Strange to say, but it's good that I know that. So thanks for the heads-up."

Chapter 16

WE called the Stallards about the helmet and the arm piece. They were happy for us and eager to examine them but couldn't come down until their spring break in early March.

Over the next few weeks, I ate like a tick stuck on a big dog, gaining back the twenty pounds I'd lost in Gilead. Except for sensitivity to cold in my left foot, my body recovered. I decided—against the wishes of my mom and the coach—not to go out for track in the spring. They weren't happy, but I had good reasons. For one, I couldn't afford to show up on the sports page of *The Magdeline Messenger* on the outside chance that the New York Jewelers guy had an interest in small-town track.

I hung my hopes on the big contrast between that clean-cut "missing boy" on the front page of the Christmas edition and the shaggy hick who'd showed up in his store with a priceless diamond. I got a haircut and cleaned up my act.

Another reason I had to pass on sports: I kept the red diamond taped to my person at all times and didn't want it ripped off in the school locker room. Every morning in the hallway at school, Rob and I would exchange baseball-type signals, and I'd tell him without a word where it was: navel, underarm, back of the neck, behind the knee, in the shoe.

I didn't walk Main Street much anymore except to stop in at Florence's for early morning grits. If nosy strangers were to show up in town asking about jewelry, I'd hear it first from the Romeos.

The clan decided to stash the armor in The Castle's attic again. I hated to part with it, but it would be safer there.

As my outer world in Magdeline closed in, my inner world grew like gangbusters. I read from the Quella every morning and night. When the weather warmed a little, I took my new leather Bible and the belt of truth back to Gilead to make peace with what happened. But I made sure to tell Dad where I was. I thanked El-Telan-Yah for the life lessons. There would be no hideout in Gilead—that much was clear. If the Day of Evil came, I'd be in the thick of it, not holed up under a rock.

I came back to camp with good news about the racers. Over twenty mixed in with other breeds had been resting in a big writhing pile above my head. Bo and a couple of naturalists did the retrieval. I'd had my fill for a while. But I got the payoff. My next plane ticket—wherever my destination—would be paid for.

Reece and I talked deep Bible stuff over lunch and didn't care who listened.

Seeing the sparks flying between Reece and me, Emma moved on to greener pastures.

Now that he was a true believer, Rob went crazy on sword research. We had Dowland's journals but figured they'd be no good. If the old man had found the sword, someone would have known. He wouldn't have kept it to himself. The journals got more random and disconnected as he reached his later years. Stanford Dowland, minister of Old Pilgrim Church, had lost the true meaning of having the armor of God. He had drifted over to the dark side until nothing was left of him but a gray, bitter wasteland. I'd gotten a taste of that a few weeks back and didn't want to go there ever again. Think like Dowland? No thanks.

The night before the Stallards came, I lay awake with the diamond held to the light, its beautiful red color and perfect shape hypnotizing me. *What's it worth? Where'd it come from? Who hid it in the helmet, and why? They could have sold it—maybe for a million bucks. Hey, I could be a millionaire! Me!*

I made a mental list of all the good I could do with the money: help Dad with the camp's debts; get Reece the best doctor in the world; buy myself a car; buy cars for Rob and Marcus and Reece too; fly Mei to Ohio for the summer; fly us all back to Leap Castle. I dreamed of all the things I could do with my fortune.

But what if . . . what if . . . the treasure has been the Stallards' goal all along? What if we're not talking thousands for the armor but millions for the diamond?

Old doubts returned—with a bigger price tag attached.

This time Aunt Grace didn't mess with the whole froufrou Victorian stuff, and we didn't have to gussy up.

The four of us met in Rob's room ahead of time and prayed about what to do.

Marcus led. "We're walking blind, Lord, walking blind. You promised to be a lamp to our feet and a light to our path. We claim it, Jesus! We're claimin' it, mighty Lord! You entrusted us with a treasure. Now we're trusting you to tell us what do."

We decided only to tell the Stallards if we felt unanimous about it.

Dr. Eloise came bursting into the Wingate Tea Room, hugged me hard, and fawned over me for surviving the ordeal. When she heard that I'd named the place Gilead, she burst into a lecture: "East of the Jordan River—the home of the first Elijah! A wild and rugged place it was in his time: hills of shaggy forests, awful solitude, dashing mountain streams, the haunt of fierce beasts! Only the hardiest sheepherders eked out a living from their stone hut settlements. To the sophisticated city dwellers in Jerusalem, the Gileadites were as unsavory as their geography—wild, uncultured, unkempt." She patted my shoulder. "He kidnapped you, didn't he?"

"Who?"

She smiled. "He's allowed. Not the best accommodations from what I heard, but you came back strong. That's often his way. He's forming a core of steel in there." She pecked on my chest with her finger. "Core of steel."

Dr. Dale shook my hand, his little old eyes looking deeply at me. He seemed unable to find any words.

As the others got seated, I asked him quietly, "Did the police question you about my disappearance?"

"They did."

"Any sign of Cravens? Are we still . . . under the radar?"

He smiled. "For now."

"And did you send Donovan?"

"Yes. Now let's have breakfast."

The clan endured me telling my war story again, each throwing in their parts about the prayer and the failed manhunt. I kept it short.

Munching scones and raspberry Danish pastries, I casually led into the subject Dom had told us about: a global network of hiding places prepared for the Day of Evil. I asked the Stallards, "Say, a while back you were talking about missionaries in The Window, how it's dangerous and kind of like spy work. I was wondering . . . if a missionary goes into The Window—or anywhere in the world—and gets into trouble there, what will he do?"

Dr. Eloise clacked her teacup down. "First, the code word is *seraph*. We don't openly call anyone in The Window a missionary. It's simply too dangerous."

"Seraph?" I asked.

"An angel of fire, a messenger from the throne of Heaven to the earth below. Our knowledge of the actual beings is scant. Around 740 BC Isaiah the prophet saw the Lord on a throne, high and exalted. Above the throne were six-winged seraphs calling out to each other, 'Holy, holy,

holy is the LORD Almighty; the whole earth is full of his glory.'" Dr. Eloise's voice rose in an arch of drama. "Their voices shook the *very walls* of the temple!" She looked at us with anticipation. "You might imagine that Isaiah was an emotional wreck at such a sight!"

"But he wasn't," I piped up.

"Oh, but he was! And to make matters worse, here came a seraph—a six-winged glowing creature—with a live burning coal from the altar of God and touched it to Isaiah's mouth!"

"Ouch!" Rob said sympathetically.

She smiled. "Growing pains, children. The coal signified that Isaiah's mouth had been cleansed from sinful talk. He was ready to grow up and be a spokesman of God." When the Lord said, 'Whom shall I send? And who will go for us?' Isaiah could answer with confidence, 'Send me!'

"All we know of seraphs is that they are fiery creatures equipped with pairs of wings to cover their faces and feet and a pair of wings to fly on divine missions."

I frowned thoughtfully. "Fiery creatures with wings, huh?" I snuck a glance at Reece. She smiled back.

"Isaiah's response to this meeting with a seraph was simply to say, 'I am undone,' or in your youth terminology, 'I am dead meat.' Seraphs are holy, powerful creatures who have a part in delivering the message before it's too late. So we call our missionaries seraphs. Please do likewise in the future." She sighed happily. "Aren't these scones just precious? I'd ask for the recipe except I rarely bake."

"Um," I tried again, "but what would a seraph do if he got in trouble?"

She dusted crumbs from her chin. "Run, hide, stand: whatever God tells him to do. It would depend on the circumstance and God's timing."

"Hide where?" Reece pried.

Dr. Eloise referred the question to her husband. "What would you say, dear?"

"Any of a number of places." He turned to Rob and changed the subject, "Did we hear correctly that you made a public confession of faith in Jesus as your Savior."

"Yes, sir, I did. I'm in."

The Stallards didn't make eye contact, but they both made nice sounds of approval over the breakfast pastries.

THE Stallards followed us up two long flights of steps for a look at the helmet.

There in the dim, dusty light of the attic stood the polished armor. The helmet hovered above the breastplate, right arm, belt, and shield, which all seemed to be floating above the shoes. It was as if an invisible warrior were standing ready. Reece gasped. It took a second to register with me that Rob had draped one of the mannequins with black cloth and hung the armor on it. It looked awesome.

We circled around it. Dr. Dale said, "Nice presentation, Mr. Wingate. Very nice."

"I polished it with a soft cloth, being careful not to scratch it."

I watched the Stallards like a hawk, searching their faces, waiting to see if they'd look under the nosepiece, so I'd know if they'd known all along there was a treasure within the treasure. Dr. Eloise whipped out a notebook and pen. "Analysis of the helmet: bronze, a variation of early Greek style. Six strips of steel meet at the top, obviously a later addition."

Rob said, "It's just like the sketch Mei made for you. See the lines etched in the metal and how they arch around, connecting every other end of the steel braces." He took the helmet off the dummy. "Look at it from the top. It makes a kind of flower or star design."

Dr. Dale commented that it looked like the ceiling of a European cathedral, but which one he couldn't remember.

Dr. Eloise went on. "An ornate band circles the head. The band has gold and silver overlays and is engraved with vines and leaves."

I said, "The short spikes sticking out in different directions are the crown of thorns. Those red globs—"

"Enamel, I believe," said Dr. Eloise.

"That's Jesus' blood."

I stepped back when they looked at the nosepiece. Rob explained how the omega, which didn't fit with the earlier style of Greek letters, meant the end. Finally Dr. Dale noticed the inside of the nosepiece. "Looks like a piece was broken off."

Rob offered the little square of chain mail. "Here. We think it was compressed and fastened there. It fits." He demonstrated.

Dr. Eloise made a note. "Extra reinforcement for the forehead? Hardly seems necessary. Hmm." She made a note about how the sides and back were designed to protect the neck. She looked at it inside and out, commented on the murky smell of the lining, and asked Marcus about the retrieval from the lake. We talked about the symbolism, and they told the story of Jesus' death on the cross.

"Notice how elegantly simple they are," she said, "the

story and the armor. No gratuitous gore recounted in the text, none of the appalling, haggard depictions you see on crucifixes; nothing of the depth of humiliation and agony our beloved Lord suffered. Yet the death is fully revealed in words and leather and metal: how he was falsely accused, convicted, stripped, whipped, crowned, mocked, spit on, taunted by enemies, abandoned by friends, nailed to a board, and pierced. Exquisitely precise, isn't it? No fluff, just fact."

I said quietly, "When I was trapped out there in Gilead, like a bug in a biology exhibit, I thought about things like that: how it must have been . . . for him."

Dr. Dale put a comforting hand on my shoulder. "How much more humiliating if everyone in Magdeline had been watching, laughing at you, leaving you there to suffer, your loved ones standing by helpless."

The idea made my skin crawl.

Reece said fiercely, "But nobody gave up."

I touched the crown of thorns, the red brads in the breastplate symbolizing the wounds in his hands and feet, the spear in his side. "They gave up on him, didn't they?"

Dr. Eloise said, "Yes, they did. They went back to their lives, certain their dreams had been dashed."

Dr. Dale examined the left shoulder of the breastplate. "You haven't found the left arm, I suppose."

Marcus said, "No sign at the bottom of Silver Lake. I doubled back twice. I'm ninety-five percent sure it's not down there."

"Maybe the arm is with the sword," Reece suggested.

I shook my head, "The sword would be with the right hand."

"Unless God's left-handed," she argued with a grin.

Dr. Eloise clucked. "Not to anthropomorphize the Almighty too much, but I daresay our creator is ambidextrous."

We went on thinking about where the missing left arm might be.

Dr. Dale said thoughtfully, "A reference in Isaiah . . . about his holy arm. Marcus, if your Quella is handy?"

"Mine's here," I said eagerly, "and with fresh batteries." I punched in the words *holy arm* and read: "'The LORD will lay bare his holy arm in the sight of all the nations, and all the ends of the earth will see the salvation of our God.'"

"Yes, of course," Dr. Dale said. He moved beside the armored mannequin to demonstrate. "See, I am extending the right hand of fellowship to my friend." He shook my hand. "But in war that same right hand fights the enemy." He detached the shield from Rob's model and held it in his left hand. Wielding an invisible sword with his right, he re-enacted a sword fight. "See here. We, the soldiers for Christ, must wear the shield of faith, traditionally on the left arm, while we hold the sword in the right. Any ideas about why the left arm might be missing?"

"I know!" said Reece. "When we stand shoulder to shoulder with our shields of faith side by side, our left arms are protected by each other."

"You still need your left arm to hold the shield," Rob said.

"But not the arm piece covering it," Reece argued.

"Good point. Here's another idea: we humans need the shield of defense. But when God comes to judge the earth, he will have no need to defend himself. He will come brandishing the sword—unconquerable, impervious to injury—leveling every foe in his path. No need of a shield. The devastation will be utterly one-sided. Symbolically we might say he will lay bare his holy arm in sudden and complete annihilation."

Dr. Dale put his hand on the shoulder of the armor as if to lean on a friend for support. Nearly whispering he said, "Imagine what it will be when the power that created the universe pinpoints his wrath on one tiny blue planet hanging on nothing in the cosmos."

The dusty air in the attic seemed to stir and quiver. I half expected the armor to move. It was the coolest kind of eerie.

Marcus said firmly, "Those demon hoards will never know what hit 'em."

Dr. Eloise whispered, "We must pray, children . . . we must . . . warn the people."

"One more piece, and we'll have the whole set," I said with conviction.

Dr. Eloise smiled sadly. "Dear Elijah. We have exhausted our resources on the matter. The trail on the sword went cold ages ago."

"I'm not giving up. Going into battle without your weapon is a suicide mission."

Rob said in a scholarly way, "My research suggests possibly Serpent Mound just south of here. The opposite of the Word of God is the silence of evil. I looked for a place of dormant evil."

"Like Leap Castle," I offered.

Reece said, "The opposite-clue thing was Dowland's idea. He never found the sword, so it can't be in an opposite place."

Rob kept on. "It makes sense that the sword would be hidden in a place that has nothing good to tell us. Like that throne of Satan in a museum in Europe."

"Or Leap," I insisted, wondering if the owl hovering over me in Gilead was a sign.

There was a lull in the conversation. The Stallards sat tiredly on the wrecked Victorian couch, looking like a faded portrait from days gone by. I felt sorry for them, driving so far, working so hard. I looked at the others for a final word about the diamond. *Do we tell them?* my eyes asked. It was unanimous. I said to the Stallards, "So that's the end of the trail for every secret of the armor. There are no more secrets?"

Dr. Eloise sighed. "Well, there is another, but it is so fantastical that we hardly dare to mention it." She looked at Dr. Dale. "By which of its names shall we call it: the Stone of Abel, the Tear of Blood, the Netsach Prism? We've long assumed it was myth born to explain the Hindu practice of—"

"I have it," I interrupted.

They stopped dead.

I had transferred it from my navel to my pocket when no one was looking. I proudly held it out in my palm. "The red diamond."

They stared in disbelief. "How . . . where?" murmured Dr. Eloise.

"It was in the nosepiece encased in clay and overlaid with metallic paint. I only found it because it had soaked in the lake for the last year. That little piece of chain mail with the encrypted verse had been fastened over it."

I let them examine it. Pressing their wrinkled cheeks together, they stood and held the red stone to the light, their eyes glittering.

Rob added, "You guys said the root word meant 'dug out.' So the treasure had to be dug out of the helmet. Pretty smart, huh?"

Dr. Dale looked at his wife. "Dear heart! Could it . . . is it . . . and if it is, what gemologist can be trusted to confirm its authenticity?"

"Oh, I don't know!" Her breathing shuddered. "No one!"

"Uh," I winced, "I already took it to someone."

Their eyes drifted from each other and rested on me, wide and fearful.

"I'm sorry, but I'd never heard of a red diamond. I thought it was glass. Doesn't it look like a hunk of old necklace or a piece from a chandelier?"

Dr. Eloise came over to me, folded my hand in hers as if to comfort me, and asked point blank, "Who knows?"

"New York Jewelers, the business that moved in when The Roanoke got blown away."

"And what did they say to you . . . when they saw it?"

"He wanted to buy it, made three offers, the biggest one being a thousand dollars. He kept wanting to take it to the back room to show his associate, said he'd be glad to recut it and put it in a piece of jewelry for me."

She nodded. "Aha! The old switcheroo. But you were not fooled."

"He tried to get my name."

"But you didn't!" Dr. Eloise froze. "Did you?"

"I told him my family was from Georgia and I was known in some parts as George Telanoo."

Reece cackled and scolded, "Elijah! Where are you known as George Telanoo?"

"Dublin," I said sort of shyly. "At that little church meeting I went to. After the run-in with Cravens, I got skittish about tossing my name around." I asked Dr. Dale, "Is that lying? I don't want to lie, but you guys don't use your real names, so I thought maybe it'd be okay."

He explained, "It's a gray area, children. We were advised early on for the sake of the mission; there are drawbacks, certainly, but we take comfort in the knowledge that angels often appear incognito when necessary and for the ultimate good. Even Jesus hid his true identity until the proper time."

"Where will you be keeping the stone?" Dr. Eloise asked me.

Rob opened his mouth to answer, but I beat him to it. "I move it to a new location every day for maximum security. It's my fault that the news is out; I take full responsibility for keeping it safe."

For a long moment, Dr. Eloise sat on the couch with the diamond nestled in her frail hand, shaking her head in disbelief. "Of all the mythic tales about the armor, I was sure this one could not be real. It has been called the Tear of Blood for obvious reasons, the Stone of Abel from the murder of Adam's son at the hands of his brother Cain. God called from Heaven, "Your brother's blood cries out to me from the ground." God does not let bloodguilt go unpunished. The blood of his people speaks across the ages and will cry out in one voice at the end. So says the prophet Isaiah. Netsach refers to the winepress of wrath in Isaiah 63." She quoted: "'Who is this, robed in splendor, striding forward in the greatness of his strength?'"

Dr. Dale answered, "'It is I, speaking in righteousness, mighty to save.'"

"'Why are your garments red, like those of one treading the winepress?'" she asked.

He responded, "'I have trodden the winepress alone; from the nations no one was with me. I trampled them in my anger and trod them down in my wrath; their blood spattered my garments, and I stained all my clothing. For the day of vengeance was in my heart, and the year of my redemption has come.'"

Dr. Dale faced the armor and said another verse: "'I will make your forehead like the hardest stone, harder than flint. Do not be afraid of them or terrified by them.'" He told us, "This verse was the one clue we believed. But since the word for hard stone—*adamant*—can also mean 'sharp,' it seemed likely that the crown of thorns was the answer. Now that we see the stone really exists, wisps of stories throughout the ages converge. Hindus have legends of sacred rivers where red diamonds are found. We may deduce that this stone came from India and at some point in history was implanted in the armor. The Hindu practice of wearing a red dot between the eyes as a symbol of sacrifice and sacred service derived from this singular pure red diamond, probably dating from the earliest centuries BC."

Dr. Eloise looked lovingly at the stone. "Oh, the lessons in one tiny stone! They say a diamond is transparent. But one can't see through it entirely because it is always reflecting back at you. And it is a stone of judgment; how one behaves as owner of such a gem says much about his character."

Dr. Dale went on, "Made from the earth's mantle, born of fire, diamonds are rugged, created to survive in the most hostile environments. The red diamond is a superstone. The properties which make it unbreakable also make it beautiful. Such is the warrior. His hardships make him strong."

They both smiled at me. Dr. Eloise said, "You are

different now, aren't you, Elijah? Your trial has toughened you?"

I nodded.

She put the Tear of Blood in my hand without a second thought, no trembling, no greedy fingers, no trying to talk me out of it like the jeweler did. "You will become stronger still. Children, surely you have already deduced that this stone is the only one of its kind known to exist. Unfortunately, the tantalizing news is out. The Tear of Blood is a holy grail, not just of the gem world, but of the antiquities world, and symbolically of the spirit world . . . for the blood of Jesus is indestructible, shed in agony, beyond worth, still crying out from Jerusalem where it was poured out, still changing the course of history to its fiery conclusion.

"This little rock will be more sought after than Noah's ark or the lost ark of the covenant from Old Testament times. The armor of God with all its parts is not just a New Testament treasure. It spans all millennia, from the cherubim's sword in the garden to the mantle of Elijah to the timeless *omen* belt—all eras all at once. It cannot be catalogued, carbon-dated, typified, or classified. It is not meant to be displayed but *used*."

Marcus had been quiet, leaning against the wall with his arms crossed. "We're targets now, aren't we? Why didn't you tell us about the diamond before? about the risks involved in finding the armor?"

Dr. Dale's head dropped sadly. "We didn't entirely

believe the myth. And why send you children searching for a fictional jewel or continue the quest out of wrong motives as Mr. Dowland apparently did?"

I agreed. "For him it became about getting rich and getting even."

Dr. Eloise added, "And nothing of the Spirit. We didn't want anything standing in the way of the real quest. So," she clapped her hands together under her chin, "the jeweler knows of the mythic stone. If he is foolish enough to let the word out, which he might be, then you must each keep a bag packed and your passports at the ready. Keep eyes and ears open." She smiled at me, "And stay out of the headlines if at all possible."

"I already quit track. So . . . um, what is the Tear of Blood worth, do you think?" I kept a steady voice.

"Would you offer it to the highest bidder?" she asked.

"No."

"Would you sell if off, dismembering the armor of God for personal gain?"

"No."

"Then your question is purely academic."

Chapter 18

SPRING was in the air. Things in my life had gone back to normal except that everything had changed. Rob stayed busy but was quieter than usual. I went through classes, sometimes in a daze, wondering what our futures held next. And the tiny stone I carried on my body began to feel as heavy as that slab in Gilead. It was on my mind every minute of the day.

First thing almost every morning at school, Rob would ask, "Where is it?" and I'd say, "Left shoe," or point to my armpit or navel. But after a while, I just couldn't hack the burden of having it with me every minute. So I made stash places: a tiny pocket on the back of the Indian blanket hanging in my room, a geode that I'd cracked open and sat next to my arrowhead collection, the knothole in the highest log on my wall, and so on.

I made a list of the stash places on an index card and had a paper clip pointing to the day's location so I wouldn't forget where I put it. That way if something happened to me, Rob would be able to find it. We had a pact.

Marcus was more withdrawn and moody. He was tired of waiting on God—like I had been before my week in Gilead. He still liked Miranda, but I now knew why he kept it cool with her. She wasn't a believer—I understood why that makes all the difference.

Emma had glommed onto Greg Moline after he won the motorcycle. So Reece and I hung out over lunch every day. I helped her with her tray and books and stuff, and nobody gave me grief.

People at school looked at me differently—partly because of my sermon that day in assembly but mostly because I'd lived though a week in the wild. I was unofficially dubbed Most Likely to Survive of the freshman class. Sometimes they'd ask to see the Quella or want to know what it was really like out there when I was trapped. I was still learning; God was still teaching me his thousand lessons.

Spring dragged on until early May when things started to change quickly. I spotted Marcus with a letter in his hand, pacing like a panther in front of my locker. I hadn't seen him so unnerved since he'd crawled on his belly to the edge of the Cliffs of Morte.

He met me halfway down the hall. "They really cut to the chase this time." He snapped the letter open and read quietly as we walked.

Children,

Our worst fears are confirmed. Your foolish jeweler believed he could quietly inquire in the diamond community about the stone. The industry is abuzz, with word rapidly spreading to the antiquities circuit. Be on your guard! Our contacts in Dublin tell us Cravens has been in a fever since our visit. After that fateful meeting, we must face the appalling truth that there is an information leak in our network. No one else to our knowledge had believed in the armor of God outside our circle, or cared to search for it. We must wonder how Dowland knew.

(By the way, Elijah, when we meet again might we get a sampling of your blood? We are a bit curious about your lineage— as you are—regarding Native American roots. Your mother, we hear, is not having much luck on her side of the family tree either. Perhaps our genealogist can help.)

Marcus grinned at me. "They want your blood." Then he went back to reading:

But back to the crisis at hand. Cravens's motives are clearly greed and fame. His feeble institute struggles to stay afloat; they need funding. Such is the case with many relic hunters worldwide. As for the diamond market, the existence of the stone has rocked the establishment.

As if we need further complication, those in the field of spiritual warfare believe the discovery of the armor is significant—one of many signs of end times. We must take great care of it for the time being so that its lessons will not be lost.

There is an upcoming conference of our core people in a location and time yet to be determined. With your permission we would like to take the armor. All of you may accompany us—of course.

We've submitted our resignations at the university and are moving our office to another city in order to be more liquid, financially and geographically. Thankfully we are not homeowners.

I interrupted him. "Wait a minute. They're going into hiding?"

"Sounds like it." He read on:

Don't be anxious for us. We're entering the next chapter of our lives, as are you.

Elijah, since the stone has been singularly connected to you (so cleverly disguised as the unkempt George Telanoo from Georgia!), we are—how shall we put this?—discussing what to do with you should things take a sudden turn. You made it clear to the jeweler that you were not interested in selling. Your evasive behavior surely piqued his attention. You, first and foremost, must keep a keen eye on your surroundings.

We don't suppose you speak any other languages, do you? Marcus, could you be of any help here?

Marcus looked up from the letter and chuckled, "How's the Latin coming along?"

I snorted. *"Cadens asinus undique portat nuper caseum."*

He shrugged. "Sounds pretty good. What's it mean?"

"The falling donkey on all sides carries recently cheese."

He gave me a look.

"I forgot to study for today's quiz. Abner almost had a stroke. Called me the most pitiable of linguists in her tenure. I don't even know what that means, and it's English. I'm not a man of words."

"You got that right."

Rob walked up and peeked over Marcus's shoulder. "What's up? Hey, a letter from the Stallards? Cool!"

Marcus went back to reading:

True, we could sell the gem and be done with it. But then we expose ourselves and the armor to the world. So, you ask, since our relic is not the actual spiritual armor we will wear in upcoming battles, why not just turn the thing over anonymously to a museum?

We cannot answer that question except to repeat that the armor may have stories yet to tell us. And—as much as we hesitate to mention it—there remains the gnawing issue of the missing sword. We have no words either of comfort or hope.

Finally, if you hear of trouble from our sector, disavow all knowledge of us and press on. The Almighty will lead you. However, do contact us if you see anything suspicious in your area. We'll send news of our whereabouts when we get settled. Above all, be strong and courageous. Angels of fire hover near, seen and unseen; seraphs fly to and fro worldwide. We can spirit you away in a matter of hours if need be. But in the end, the quest will be yours. You children began it, and you must carry it to its certain conclusion. We'll keep you posted.

Traveling light,
The Stallards

"'Certain conclusion?' What certain conclusion?" Rob asked.

"I think they mean God's plan," Marcus answered flatly. "We follow blind."

Before the week had passed, Reece heard from Mei. I knew something was up when she grabbed me in the hall and shoved me into our corner. "I don't know what this means," she said shakily. "In Devo club we keep coming across Scriptures about the islands. 'Be silent before me, you islands! Let the nations renew their strength! Let them come forward and speak; let us meet together at the place of judgment.' 'The islands will look to me and wait in hope.' And then I hear this quiet voice in my heart saying, *You need to go there. You need to go there.* So I'm thinking, sure okay, Lord—one of these days. Then I got this!" She pulled a letter from her purse. It was from Mei.

"Hold it," I said. "This is for the whole clan."

Running ahead of the pack after school (it was raining, so Reece and the guys got a ride), I headed into Florence's but had to make a quick U-turn when I spotted the New York Jewelers guy buying coffee. I ran back outside, leaped into their back seat, and said, "Change of plans. Tree House Village!"

Like in the good old days, we gathered with camp snacks and hid ourselves away high in the feathery, light green trees of spring. Reece read Mei's letter:

Dear Reece, Elijah, Rob, and Marcus,

How are you? I am doing well. Thank you again for my Trinity ring. I wear it every day and remember my best friends. School is very hard. I am jealous that you will be out in a few weeks!

We have had a few earthquakes lately. Most are small, but one lasted many seconds and was scary!

I have been reading the Bible, and I have many questions. But I do believe in Jesus. His story is true! I didn't understand that the time of all history is divided on the life of Jesus—BC and AD. Until I met you, I thought Jesus was a hero from fairy tales like Hercules. But he is real. I love to read about him very much. He was kind and strong.

Is he like my friends in Magdeline? I think so a lot.

I have found a church in my village. It is different from your big American church. It is very small, and the people have many struggles. I now see how dark and sad my village is. Our valley is a beautiful place with friendly people. But their lives are hopeless. People live with much fear. We pray to small gods, but it is just wishing. People are afraid of oni—*demons. Everyone goes to temples and shrines. It is just custom but so hard to leave. The family is very hurt if I stop the customs!*

When I started to read the Bible, God woke me up!

Please come and help me show my friends the love and power of God like you did for me. Thank you, Reece, for being my best friend. Thank you, Elijah, for saving my life. Thank you, Marcus and Rob, for being cool guys who will spend time with the gaijin *girl.* Arigatou gozaimasu! *Thank you very much!*

I want to come to Magdeline this summer, but I cannot. I must study! But if you come to my home, I am indebted to be a good hostess. This is important to Japanese people! Please come and rescue me from study!

Greetings to Stallards and all your nice parents.

Love and peace,

Mei Aizawa

PS. I know it costs a lot for you to come. If you cannot, it is okay. But I am reading the Bible, and I don't understand so much.

"He put on righteousness as his breastplate, and the helmet of salvation on his head; he put on the garments of vengeance." Then it said, "So will he repay wrath to his enemies . . . he will repay the islands their due." It makes me worried that God will use his armor against me because I live on an island. Can you explain to me? Can you help me?

Thank you, Reece. I love you all.

Reece crushed the letter to her heart. "We have to go! We have to!"

I said, "Sure. Okay." But I was thinking, *Impossible!*

I sat on the steps of Mag High. It was an hour before classes started, but that morning I couldn't sleep. *Three weeks until I can shut the door to Abner's class forever. Three weeks to freedom: campfires, working with Dad, night hikes and owl calls, nature walks through Council Cliffs, hanging out with the clan, and climbing Great Oak again . . . with Reece . . . maybe.*

I held the Tear of Blood in my fist.

Reece got dropped off by her mom. She came up, sat down beside me, glanced at my closed hand, and made a sarcastic face. "Is that where you're hiding it today?"

I opened my fingers enough for her to see the diamond. It picked up the sun's rays and glowed. "I don't know what to do with it. Rob was right; duct tape is very bad for your skin." I didn't tell her I'd worn raw places around my waist and under my arms. I didn't tell her that the stone was wearing out more than my skin. It was wearing my soul down.

"Did you pray about what to do?"

"Um, not yet."

"Don't forget what you learned in Gilead every day at 3:00. Prayer works."

We sat there looking at each other in the cool quiet of morning. I studied her pretty face. I noticed her gold star earrings. I reached up and pinched her earlobe. Then I pinched mine, thinking about the size and thickness.

She instantly knew what I was thinking. "Implant it? Oh, that would hurt. You'd have to get a doctor to do it. He'd think you were—"

I broke in, "A dumb kid starting a new fad."

"He probably wouldn't do it. He'd ask questions. Anyway, you can't let anyone else see the Tear of Blood. And you better not try it yourself. It would get infected and swell up."

I agreed. "I guess we won't be able to use the we're-dumb-kids excuse much longer. That's a shame. It works so well."

She grinned. "We're almost sophomores."

"Can't wait." We turned that over in our minds. Absently I felt behind my ear, the top part where the skin seemed sort of loose over the cartilage. It would be a good place. It might work . . .

She reached out her hand. "Let me see the stone. Maybe the clue for the sword is on it or in it," she said.

I shook my head. "Rob put it under a microscope."

"It's beautiful." She took it and rolled it around in her palm. "Hard to believe people would kill for it though."

I looked at her a long time. "I've gotta do something with it."

"Your nerves have to be shot. You're the only person in the world connected to it. And the guy in New York Jewelers works right down the street. You pass him every day on the way home!"

"Not anymore. I cut through yards and follow the tracks behind the bank or across the Morgan farm."

"He probably wouldn't recognize you," she said encouragingly. "You looked a lot different right after you came out of Gilead—all skinny and grungy. You've spiffed up. New clothes. Nice haircut. More muscle. She squeezed my arm and smiled. "No more looking like Dowland—what a relief!"

We got quiet. I took the gem, slipped it into the tiny leather pouch I'd made, peeled the hunk of duct tape off my ankle, and secured it in place beside my ankle bone.

I stared out across the school lawn, disheartened. "We have the armor but no weapon."

"It's symbolic. Don't forget that. You do have the Word. The Quella."

"Yeah, but . . ."

"I know." She sighed. "I'm tired of waiting too. So is Marcus. He's ready for action."

I shuddered. "Don't say that! The last time I complained about waiting on God, I ended up under a two-ton rock. Then I was *really* waiting! I say God can take *all* the time he wants! We'll deal with it."

"You know, though, looking back over the past year and a half, so much has changed, and pretty fast. Just think about it."

"Yeah. When Rob was baptized it hit me: four of my clan of five are *in*."

She nodded. "One to go: Mei. And all of the pieces are found but the last."

"One to go," I said. Hope started creeping back into my soul. Reece had that effect on me.

"Remember how we doubted every time, Elijah? We thought we'd never find a piece; then we'd find it."

"*You* didn't doubt, Reece. You never doubted."

"Sometimes I did."

Buses pulled in; kids piled out.

I stood and helped Reece up. "There's nothing we can do about the sword right now."

"But we can do something about Mei. You can complete your clan. She's ready. She needs us. And God keeps saying to me, 'You need to go there.'"

We climbed the steps and headed into Mag High. My hopes still lagging, I said to her, "Ireland's one thing, Reece. But Japan? That seems impossible."

"Impossible," she murmured with a mysterious smile. She looked up at me and chirped, "Perfect!"

THE CARPET OF BONES

IT'S been more than a year since Elijah Creek escaped Gilead by the skin of his teeth—a year of silence and uncertainty. Then suddenly the clan is caught up in a whirlwind mission of spiritual warfare through Japan. They reunite with Mei, experience her amazing culture of ninja, raw fish, mysterious mountains, and speeding bullet trains, and are initiated into the Stallards' secret global network.

Then threatening messages come in dreams and whispers from around the globe. Elijah and his friends have invaded the territory of a dark principality who has been gathering strength since the dawn of history. Elijah *has* found a sword. But is it the sword of the Lord, the weapon needed for the battle they face? Are they armed against the entity's threats? Or is the sword a fake?

Tragedy crushes the very heart of the clan. But power comes with the undeniable proof that someone is watching over them.

In the seventh and final installment of The Armor of God series, *The Carpet of Bones,* readers will see the armor of God in action, understand the path Elijah must take, and discover the destiny of the Magdeline Five.

Ancient Truth

(Page 6, 93) "The god who answers by fire—he is God."

1 Kings 18:24

(Page 13) "A sword for the LORD and for Gideon!"

Judges 7:20

(Page 77) "The Rock of Israel . . . blesses you with blessings of the heavens above, blessings of the deep that lies below."

Genesis 49:24, 25

(Page 77) "The LORD is my rock, my fortress and my deliverer; my God is my rock, in whom I take refuge. He is my shield."

Psalm 18:2

(Page 78) "Elijah was a man just like us. He prayed earnestly that it would not rain, and it did not rain on the land for three and a half years. Again he prayed, and the heavens gave rain, and the earth produced its crops."

James 5:17, 18

(Page 83, 117) "Naphtali is abounding with the favor of the LORD and is full of his blessing; he will inherit southward to the lake."

Deuteronomy 33:23

(Page 102) "Be still, and know that I am God."

Psalm 46:10

(Page 103, 106) "Even though I walk through the valley of the shadow of death, I will fear no evil, for you are with me."

Psalm 23:4

(Page 104) "In the beginning God created the heavens and the earth."

Genesis 1:1

(Page 104) "God is light; in him there is no darkness at all."

1 John 1:5

(Page 105) "Jesus answered, 'It is written: "Man does not live on bread alone, but on every word that comes from the mouth of God."'"

Matthew 4:4

(Page 106) "For our struggle is not against flesh and blood, but against the rulers, against the authorities, against the powers of this dark world and against the spiritual forces of evil in the heavenly realms."

Ephesians 6:12

(Page 129) "Then the Almighty will be your gold, the choicest silver for you."

Job 22:25

(Page 142) "A cord of three strands is not quickly broken."

Ecclesiastes 4:12

(Page 161) "And they were calling to one another: 'Holy, holy, holy is the LORD Almighty; the whole earth is full of his glory.'"

Isaiah 6:3

(Page 162) "Then I heard the voice of the Lord saying, 'Whom shall I send? And who will go for us?'"

Isaiah 6:8

(Page 167) "The LORD will lay bare his holy arm in the sight of all the nations, and all the ends of the earth will see the salvation of our God."

Isaiah 52:10

(Page 172) "The LORD said, 'What have you done? Listen! Your brother's blood cries out to me from the ground.'"

Genesis 4:10

(Page 172) "Who is this, robed in splendor, striding forward in the greatness of his strength? 'It is I, speaking in righteousness, mighty to save.' Why are your garments red, like those of one treading the winepress? 'I have trodden the winepress alone; from the nations no one was with me. I trampled them in my anger and trod them down in my wrath; their blood spattered my garments, and I stained all my clothing. For the day of vengeance was in my heart, and the year of my redemption has come.'"

Isaiah 63:1-4

(Page 173) "I will make your forehead like the hardest stone, harder than flint. Do not be afraid of them or terrified by them."

Ezekiel 3:9

(Page 181) "Be silent before me, you islands! Let the nations renew their strength! Let them come forward and speak; let us meet together at the place of judgment."

Isaiah 41:1

(Page 181) "The islands will look to me and wait in hope."

Isaiah 51:5

(Page 183) "He put on righteousness as his breastplate, and the helmet of salvation on his head; he put on the garments of vengeance. . . . So will he repay wrath to his enemies . . . he will repay the islands their due."

Isaiah 59:17,18

Creek Code

※※※

Delaware
Langundowagan—(lahn-goon-do-wah-gahn) Peace

Greek
Koinonia—Fellowship
Soterion—Salvation

Hebrew
Omen—(oh-men) Truth, faithfulness

Irish Gaelic
Cathach—(kah-thukh) Warrior
Creidim—(kred-im) Faith

Japanese
Gi—(ghee) Righteousness
Gaijin—(gah-ee-jeen) Foreigner
Arigatou gozaimasu!—(ah-ree-gah-toh go-zah-ee-mah-su)
    Thank you very much!
Oni—(oh-nee) Demon

Latin
Peregrini—(peh-reh-gree-nee) Pilgrim

Check out this other series . . .

GAME ON!

Stephen D. Smith with Lise Caldwell

GAME ON! is a
sports fiction series
featuring young athletes
who must overcome
obstacles—on and off
the field. The characters
in these stories are
neither the best athletes
nor the underdogs.
These are ordinary kids
of today's culture—
characters you'll
identify with and
be inspired by.

0-7847-1729-X

0-7847-1730-3

0-7847-1731-1

0-7847-1735-4